Someday I hope his writing is studied by kids in school. We all should have such grit and grace. His imagination is wide and vivid and words flow like water. Thank goodness for his Irish ancestry, it runs fast and thick in his blood. I'm always amazed how he puts words together, how his mind makes connections and com- parisons so glibly and astutely. And how he reaches so deeply into the most simple element and pulls out an essence from a unique point of view. Makes me want to go to that mountain and see the rise to the moon and the prairie running to it.

-Diane Buccheri, editor and publisher of
Ocean Magazine

A distinguished poet, author, and Korean War veteran, Tom Sheehan's writing is deep and moving, special! His hard-earned publishing success is impressive. His lifetime mentoring experience passing through his writing is a voice evoking Dylan Thomas's. Tom's war poems are stunning and beautiful. Many veterans will fall down crying and kiss the ground when they hear his true stories. After reading Tom's accounts of military life, I understood why my recruiter offered me a keg of rum to enlist in 1977. To me, that keg represented the 8th wonder of the world – Tom Sheehan is its 9th.

-Sally Drumm, Leader of Milspeak Creative Writing Seminars and editor of *Milspeak,* an anthology of military memoir

Tom Sheehan brings more to Saugus than one can imagine, and wrings lasting memories out of it in every word he writes. You can find pieces of Saugus in each story he creates because he will not let go of the town we both love.

-John Burns, co-editor, *Of Time and the River, Saugus 1900-2005*

i

My opinion has not changed since the first Sheehan word I read, he is an American treasure, a gifted wordsmith, and a literary icon of the highest order. Now if we could only get God to do a reading of his work, life would be perfect.

-Laurel Johnson, reviewer, *Midwest Review*

If there is anyone else out there who can spin a short story as well as he can, I've yet to find an equal to Tom Sheehan's style. I am not the only one who gets caught from the start, feels the sensually descriptive words, the warmth in them, the care in crafting, linking, and presentation to the reader, who immediately feels at home with his characters, known them forever, like old home-town friends. You don't just read a work by Tom, it works you, never leaving you alone, resonating long after. Once you read him, you'll understand. And if you are lucky enough to have lived in Saugus, you already know why he is as good at it as he is.

-Tom Weddle, Brunswick, Maine (Saugonian by birth)

From the Quickening

Thomas Sheehan

Pocol Press
Clifton, VA

POCOL PRESS

Published in the United States of America
by Pocol Press
6023 Pocol Drive
Clifton VA 20124
www.pocolpress.com

Publisher's Cataloguing-in-Publication

Sheehan, Thomas F, 1928-

    From the quickening / Thomas Sheehan. – 1st ed.
    – Clifton, VA : Pocol Press, c2009.

    p.; cm.

    ISBN 13: 978-1-929763-39-9

    1. Short stories, American. 2. American fiction. I. Title

PS3569.H39216 F76 2009
813.6--dc22   0904

Dedication

Dedicated with the utmost expectation to the newest
Sheehan in the band, the next writer in the clan, and the swiftest of
our athletes who arrives ahead of the others.

Table of Contents

Acknowledgments

With deep appreciation, the author notes those stories included here that were selected by editors of the following publications and were published in revisions presented here or in earlier versions:

Projected Letters; The Emergence of Slow Purple, Two Characters Caught up in Chapel Town, Red River Shoes

Canopic Jar, Subtle Tea; Miss Magnusson and the Druggist

Word Riot, Flask Review; Too Much Asia to Wipe Off

Muscadine Lines, Seeker; Receipt at Ogden's Twist

Nuvein; Keepsake

Hackwriters; Driving on the Sausage Run

Triplopia; Fourth of July Homecoming

Plum Ruby Review, Indite Circle, Ululation; Driving on the Sausage Run

Combat Magazine; The Unforgotten

New Works Review; The Dollhouse Victim, Miss Magnusson and the Druggist, Kommando Loose in Maine

The Dublin Quarterly; The Sentencing of Madrigal Orpic

Pindeldyboz; Caitlin, Tollgate Collector

Literary Potpourri; The Dollhouse Victim

Green Silk Journal; Sneaker on the Beach

Quickness comes with packaging; ideas on the edge, chance, excitement, a reach for the impractical, the rules of a new game with an old touch… at length, contemplation and perhaps small conversion, making it all worth it.

-Chemkin Talbus, visionary

Receipt at Ogden's Twist

Young Trace Gregson, thin and curly at eleven and generally happy-faced, cringed whenever he saw Dirty Molly Sadow. If there was such a thing as a bad witch about in the world, she was it. People said her toes were black with earth rich as The Hollow, and that she smelled foul as chicken leavings.

Now Molly walked to the Amicalola River behind her little shack with a burlap bag in her hand. Her calico dress was rotten with age and stain and gray hair hung thin as tree moss on her shoulders. The beat of a limp was in her gait. Now and then the bag bumped along the ground as if the weight was too much for her to tote. Trace thought he heard muted cries coming from her side of Ogden's Twist, this torturous turn in the Amicalola River, as he hid in the weeds on the side across from Molly. One keeper trout flattened its rainbow inside his wicker creel.

Then it hit him. Molly's bitch of a Golden Retriever, Muscatel, had been full of pups but days before, her body low with the swelling. The soft cries came to him again, almost like prayers in the front row at church, and then Molly heaved the bag into the fast part of Ogden's Twist.

The bag hit with a big splash and sank in a swirl of current. Dirty Molly walked off without looking back.

Trace, in dungarees and sneakers, leaped into the river as soon as she went behind a mound of trash. The chill of the water hit him with a crushing blow. His breath held for him. On his second drop into the swift water, he found the burlap bag. His hand closed on the soft mass. The squirming in it telegraphed up his arm. Ashore, gasping for breath, he pulled the old shoelace loose from the twisted neck of the bag and dumped the contents in the tall grass. His eyes lit up. Life plummeted out! Five Golden Retriever pups spilled onto the grass. A sixth fell out and lay still. Trace felt his own heart bang in his chest.

Leaving the dead pup and his gear on the bank of Ogden's Twist, he rushed off to the most reliable and kindest man he had known in his short life, Uncle Jack Parlee, a retired mailman. Living alone, Jack kept a small garden on the river, this side of Ogden's Twist, a small garage notorious for its collection of old

1

tools, and two old and labored hounds who were bent and slow in their years. Nameless, he simply called them *my old boys*.

As Trace knew it would happen, the salvaged pups were given a new home in a corner of the porch. The sun streamed in there at crazy angles at different parts of the day. Some days, by the rays, he could tell the hour or see his growth pattern on the wall. Trace could always sense the warmth of the porch. Jack promised nothing, but set straight away at continuing the salvage. He patted his nephew on the back of his head. "You got heart, boy. Momma did you good." Trace's father had died five years earlier in a late night truck crash on the main highway west of the Amicalola. He and his mother now lived alone in their house.

Trace returned to get his fishing gear and to bury the dead pup. The sun was getting back a piece of his body, touching him reverently. For a brief moment he felt the thanks in it and the quick needles. A lone cloud sailed along at the bright horizon against Storm Mountain. He decided that at any second the cloud and the mountain top would collide. He'd be too far away to hear the crash. Still a long walk from his gear, he heard the howling and abated fury of a dog. For sure, he thought, it was Muscatel trying to reclaim her pups. At the banking of the river, Trace heard Muscatel's baying cry. It sounded like a friend's mother calling home her children just as darkness came filtering over the horizon.

Then Muscatel hove around the trash pile behind Dirty Molly's house. Her nose was bent to the ground and she was howling weirdly. The noise caught up in Trace's chest. It made his heart beat with a new tempo. He felt as if he had just come up from another dive in the cold water.

Muscatel stood at the water's edge, her quandary evident to the sole onlooker. She stood as lonely as Trace Gregson had ever seen loneliness stand. The water moved swiftly, the beautiful Golden Retriever, like a statue, stuck her head into the air above the river. From where he sat in the reeds and tall grass, Trace believed she was measuring distance or possibility, or both. He knew he could not move her from that spot, could not drag her.

The cloud and the mountain went their way, silent and distant. The water of the Amicalola and Ogden's Twist, here and there turbulent, continued on its rush to the sea miles away.

2

Butterflies, though silent as smoke, punctuated the air against a deep green background of leafy trees, and the hum of bees and birds came as softly as a new engine.

The parallels slowly came to Trace Gregson in the days that followed.

"Them pups sure is pretty, Trace. Bet they grow like weeds from now on. Hate to have them loose in my beans and corn. They'd grow me under." His Uncle Jack sat on the rocker on the porch. "You keep an eye on that hag of a woman, that dog of hers, too, she ever leaves her watch. And if she gets fat again, you got more swimming to do."

And for weeks on end he saw Muscatel standing at the river, no longer baying out over the water, but watching, distance and possibility still crowding the air. Trace fished every day on his side of the river and thought about the widow's peaks his uncle had told him about that he had seen in parts of Maine and in New Bedford. "Lookout women waiting for their husbands' ships. 'Bout as patient as you can get," he said, "but needing a sure view of what was going on, what might happen. They plain last saw their man there, hoping to see him again at the same place." He thought the hapless mother would never leave her *peak*. Uncle Jack made no suggestions to that consideration.

It was months later, the pups sturdy as rocks, thick in the chest, bearing names he and Uncle Jack had conjured up out of a big collection of books, Trace saw the swelling again as it rounded Muscatel's frame. Soon after, he began a new vigil at the river. Every day he dug worms for the morning, saw Dirty Molly come evenings from the chicken farm where she worked, saw her off on the weekday mornings.

Rain had cooled the night. Morning was bright and leafy and green all the way to the mountain top. It was Saturday, his fly line floated down into the bubbling water of the river. Something in the air hit him broadside. It was the sound he had heard before, the near muted cries, the sense of loss or doom. Dirty Molly was making the same trip. On his belly, he slipped quietly through the weeds, his eye on her. Another burlap bag was in her hands. Again it bounced on the ground. Again it was heaved into the water. Again she turned away and did not look back.

The cold water hit him again. His breath hung on again, but he felt a sudden panic this time. Nothing came to hand on the first or second dive. He dove a third time, his dungaree pockets now loaded with water, his sneakers heavy, his chest ready to burst. Uncle Jack would be on the porch with the dogs. The sun would be pouring down on them, sort of holy and secret and full of goodness.

He reached through the cold darkness, now desperate.

The bag touched his hands and seemed to loop away. He dove again and found it. Dirty Molly had wound a wire loop about the knotted neck. A point of wire pricked his thumb. The jackknife was in his dungaree pocket. He scrambled ashore, the bag instantly whipped out of water, the liquid film still crowding its surface, the whole bag sealed against breathing.

The knife was sharp and cut the bag easily and five more pups, spitting water, legs still at torment, spilled from the bag. As before, he put them in his creel and hurried off to sanctuary. He wondered how many of these trips he had missed in Muscatel's life, or in the life of any other dog that Molly might have kept.

Muscatel, as before, came again for days on end to the edge of Ogden's Twist. Trace watched her in secret as she sniffed the ground, sniffed the air itself, his own heart always in riot and commotion.

"Someday, girl, you'll have your day."

The two batches of kindred pups looped their harmony. Jack kept them in the yard, now with a fence around it. Though the garden was smaller, the dogs were bigger. One of *his old boys* had passed on and was buried at the edge of Ogden's Twist.

Some nights the porch for Trace was a piece of heaven.

Then one night, as the sheriff told it, someone had slipped into Dirty Molly's shack to steal the horde of money it was said she had hidden away. Molly supposedly caught him at it and died of a heart attack. There were no bruises on her.

But Muscatel was on her own.

One morning, his fishing pole over his shoulder and his creel braced with a pair of trout, Trace and Muscatel came together on Trace's side of Ogden's Twist, that adventurous spin in the Amicalola.

4

Trace had not seen her for weeks.

"C'mon, girl," he said, "we got some catching up to do."
The two apparent strangers walked down the narrow road leading
away from the river. The occasional trees overhead were
umbrellas and loaded with warm sounds.

Trace Gregson knew the sun beating down on Muscatel
and him was holy and full of grace. The back of his neck was
warm. The warmth flooded his body. His hands felt it, and it went
scurrying the length of his arms. He whistled. Muscatel, somewhat
heavy- footed, trotted along beside him as if she were a long time
fishing pal. Jack saw them coming.

The folks at Ogden's Twist still say such a howling ensued
that day that stories could be written of it.

Night Song Singer of Broken Halleluiahs

For the third night in a row, Cavin Woodmarsh (long, lean, young, often caught up in a dream) strolled to the far end of Riverside Cemetery with a guitar over his shoulder in a case the long road had beaten up as badly as old shoes. Most things about him were soft, suitable, acceptable... the long fingers, the readily available smile, a detectable aura packing no punch other than immediate belief carried in his voice. His gait was sure, and his eyes somehow fit midnight's deep color. Hurry did not accompany him, though, or any sign of stealth. The prime silence was now and then cluttered by a post-midnight automobile on a distant road; but Cavin had earlier, on the two previous nights, found acoustical acceptance while playing the guitar beside a tall marble mausoleum where inscribed names capitulated to darkness.

This night he sat on a small stone bench, perhaps a mourner's bench he thought, and drifted further into the darkness.

Like all nights of magic, music came out the other side.

He half believed he had perfected a new song.

Soon thereafter, on the hill beside the cemetery, Sewell Grafton was sure of the odd disturbance. It was a guitar he heard, and faintly, over the chords, a word that sounded like a broken prayer. *Halleluiah* it said in soft and stretched out pieces, as if being parsed in English classes he once hated... *Ha..lay... loo... yaaaaa.* Again... *Haa..laaay... loooo... yaaaaaaa,* the syllables longer in breath, and rising uphill from old Riverside. It ran again, leaped again, carried past long breath up the slope of the hill, surmounting ledges, hardness, his ear.

If neighbors on the hill heard that one among them had called police about the lilted

Halleluiahs, they'd know it to be Sewell Grafton. A hundred to one it'd be Grafton. Two of the neighborhood women on the hill, one with a tongue loose as flannel pajamas, had reiterated what Grafton's dying wife had said on her death bed, "This is one tough way to get rid of a husband, by dying."

With a stab of decision, Sewell Grafton was on the phone to the police station. "I've had about enough of this revolutionary,

6

holier-than-thou music, this midnight crap going on. It's a disturbance of the peace, that's what it is, and I want something done about it. It's damned sacrilegious coming from the cemetery." He took in a deep breath, tried to quell the rising anger taking over his whole person, and simply said, "Now." He said it a second time, keying his intensity. "Now." He could feel the sincerity of his threat, and measured the momentary silence from the other end of the phone line. He knew he had delivered the threat even as he heard the strummer again, from below in the cemetery. "Down there in the cemetery, he's some Hippie probably licking his chops," he muttered, to the dark night in general and to no one in particular, not even to the officer on the phone.

For the second or third night in a row, July crowding him on his porch, the trees alive, the flowers leaking into the sweltering heat coming to him from the nearby cemetery, only minor uncertainties in the air, Grafton had thought he heard music, strumming music, chorded music, but not his kind of music if he had a kind of music to favor. Practically to the very minute of his phone call, he thought it came from a neighbor's raucous radio or television. All as if one of their kids, banging up the volume even though distant, was trying to get even with someone. Maybe out to disturb him; he'd had the thought before, though he didn't know why, never knowing what his dying wife had said when she left this world nine years before.

The music, in spite of the late hour, seemed to him also, at that same moment, to be something else. The arrows of that thought clustered clearer in his mind, as the cemetery seemed to be revealed as the source.

Here, on his piece of the Henshit Mountain above the cemetery, but really a minor hill of two hundred or so feet, Sewell, in lonely retirement for all of those nine years, sat his uneasy way on the porch for better part of most days, and often long into nights whether melodious or not. Solitude became him, thinking it was his due, that all of good silence had been earned. At these sittings he had his old daydreams. He sat with his feet up on a soft but deep red and rugged ottoman. He sometimes kept his eyes

7

closed for long minutes of deep ecstasy. He smoked cigars in spite of all threats, medical, social, and otherwise, thinking there was nothing wrong with a long, rich drag when he was alone, regardless of what it carried off or brought in upon itself in exchange. Silence, after all the harsh sounds of his life, was often one beautiful thing… it touched what he thought was his soul… his belief extending that far. It calmed him. His last ten years of work as a telephone solicitor, collecting the garbage of pennies for many causes, had colored his vision of life. Silence was his due… no more excuses, no lies, no hate plowing right through the ether at him. No abrupt hanging up of phones after a three minute delivery so smooth it promised to rankle no one but his own feelings in retrospect.

And now some damned Hippie out on the night!

At a repeated chord from downhill, the edge of his mind stiffened, then his jaw, and at length his backbone. Now he knew that the music was rising to grate him from the darkness of Riverside Cemetery, a plunging 100 yards down from his porch and a quick jump across Winter Street. It was, without a doubt, a guitar in the hands of some wise-ass kid.

The night desk man at the police station looked over his shoulder at Sgt. Culberson. "It's that pain in the ass again up on Henshit Mountain. Old man Sewell. Says somebody's down in Riverside Cemetery having a concert. Wants it stopped. 'Now!' he says." He rolled his eyes in accent.

Culberson rolled his eyes in answer. "I'll check it out. Be right back. Want a Duncan's?" His tall and athletic frame rose to a distinctive six feet and four inches, his eyes bright, his hair prematurely white that gave him a handsome middle life look, ladies measuring him as virile from the outset. Crinkly crows' feet made his face pleasant, thoughtful, calm. He'd been through a couple of wars of his own and wore the trappings well, as was said about him around town: "Culberson's been where some of us have never been, and hoping it stays that way."

"On you, I'll take it." The desk man's nod was both an acceptance of appreciation and one of respect.

The headlights of the cruiser knocked out a slim tunnel of darkness as Culberson started down the middle road of Riverside

8

Cemetery, the windows open as he listened for the *upstart* music. Inscribed stones, hundreds of faces marked with names, some he knew, many he didn't, flashed data at him from the edges of each plot beside the road.

In a moment, in a stab of light, the name of George Hanover thrust itself from the past. The sergeant remembered the old man whittling on the steps of the house across the street from him, the tiny wooden soldiers that old George Hanover would drop into his young hands, him a wide-eyed general with an army of troopers in his back yard, leaded ones and wooden ones, infantry and cavalry and small armored columns, and the special soldiers he painted up with true uniforms. Then, in those young days, the neatness for him was most important, more important than the uniform, but not now, his now wearing the badge, the chevrons, and the golden braid.

He shut off the engine, shut down the lights as he saw again the image of George Hanover falling over from the very same steps, a half whittled Civil War soldier squeezed in his hand, the working knife fallen somewhere at his side, his breath gone elsewhere too. The whole scene caught at his heart all anew. Distinctly, down to the tarnished blue and marked remains of the uniform as if in a photograph, he saw that one Civil War piece sitting yet on his mantel at home, the lone remnant of his young days at war on the lot-wide spread of sandy dunes in the back yard.

He let the images drift away into the darkness, that flight too he had known many times, memory a continual part of his make-up, the past often sitting the same seat with him or running around in his head, directly behind his eyeballs. The punctuation he knew and the stumble to death and had been able to read much of it since that day an old man had squeezed him dry.

Darkness, in sudden realization, had often hidden both good and bad surprises; he was prepared for either.

For long moments he heard no sound at all, no music, no strum of an instrument he thought he would be hearing, no sweet pickings. Sewell, for that matter he realized, really was a cranky old man. It was not the first time he had called the station, late at night, about some rowdiness or noise, feeling picked upon; self-appointed pariah of Henshit Mountain.

Culberson wondered at length what motivated such people, how they might measure themselves coming up in others' eyes, think what the world might think of them, if that mattered in the first place.

Cocking an ear, he turned his head sideways and stood still as a pole. The darkness thickened as though in a cake mix, all ingredients tossed in and coming up dim as chocolate, thick with promise. Some parts of music there were that he loved, could spend hours listening to: the Three Tenors, Andrea Boccelli with the fair English singer, Sarah Brightman, some guitar guys in the army that sounded as if Hank Williams senior was back at the mike, pure country with a soul echoing loss and pain, and the sad joys of love. *I'm So Lonesome I Could Cry* and *Lost Highway* took turns at revelation.

For moments he was locked into the sweetest reverie one's mind can imagine. His body grew slack, then went into a momentary lift where light and music and touch overcame him. He was home in a kind of happiness he had not felt in a long time. It was fluid. It touched his skin. It swam about him. He could taste it. But he heard no music as he tensed in apprehension. Counted breaths went their way, sly as footpads in escape.

Then, a string at a time, each a distal note, a guitar's exhalation crawled out of the darkness.

Faintly, on an upward lift of air, a zephyr of sound came to him from way down at the East Saugus end of Riverside, a scattering of notes that might have been jumbled on the air, a mix of keen sounds. Then he caught a chord of it, something soft and memorable, saying, deep inside, that he had heard it before. As quick as it had come, it faded away, as if a wind has tousled with the zephyr of air, winning the unbalanced enmity.

Culberson knew he was caught between something highly unlikable and something likable, cresting at the moment in the back of his mind as a kind of favorite from his past, an ambivalence exerting itself through the life of his senses.

10

The long-time policeman thought himself dwarfed, made meek and mild, at the discretion of gods or god-like essences he might not have known before.

Upon measurement, he thought the strummer, the picker, to be a pretty good musician, having a belief in notes and what was to follow, to be melodious, to be warm, to cover and protect him here in the absolute darkness. But he was not sure of the voice thence coming at him on a sheet of slightly moving air, a thin element of voice, one on the alto side of the ledger. Voices, he knew, those voices that become favored ones, you had to warm up to, had to embrace, whether by repetition of favored songs, by the poetry they carried or by a story from their words, or else, by chords so beautiful and plentiful on the ear, they would not leave you in any hurry, words you could hum into music, remember like a fond face, a fair glance at beauty itself.

The far voice transmitted itself, reached, found a new level where warmth accompanied each following note, and ran the chords into a touching beauty.

Now, in this place, in this space, he was an in-between-er, struck and stuck there betwixt the new and the old, the moving and the sedate, the fresh and the stale. This night, he said to himself so as not to disturb the sounds reaching him, was at a critical juncture.

He had no idea of who the musician was, what he looked like, or what had happened earlier in the Center, when the beat officer, from his cruiser, spotted the tall young man walking slowly down the street with a guitar case slung by a hunk of rope over one shoulder. He had not recognized the late walker. Had not seen him before. Finding curiosity and wonder yanking at him for answers, he pulled the cruiser beside the young man.

"You from around here, son? I haven't seen you before. Where you heading? Get a late start home? Need a lift?" Cautiously, he looked around to check if anybody else was about. Nothing but harmless shadows hovered in places.

"I was supposed to meet a pal and we were going to practice a few songs, but he never showed. I'm new here, living with my aunt and uncle on Winter Street for the time being.

11

The gray cape with the porch screens still leaning against the house, like they've been all year, maybe a couple of years." A slight smile warmed his face. "I promised I'd put them up, for my uncle, Ned Garvey. Know him?"

"I know the place, and know him. Good luck on that. I hope they're in good shape. They sure are kind of a landmark on the street. What's your name, son?" The policeman's voice had warmed up.

"Cavin."

"Any good on that thing?" he said, as he pointed to the guitar case.

"I can celebrate a lot of things with it, including freedom and deep thought."

The patrolman on wheels felt himself caught in place. He nodded and released the foot brake, easing away from the young man. "Good luck, kid. I mean it." Shortly he had a Bruce Springsteen song on his radio, a night rider and cohort in dark patrol.

Culberson knew none of this that had happened a bit earlier, even as he decided to lock up the cruiser and proceed on foot to where the music was coming from. His memory gave him a quick shot of a marble mausoleum, a stone bench, and the chain link fence that marked the end of the cemetery. He marked where the house of an old teacher of his was still painted pale blue on the other side of the chain link fence. Names of a few pals, now and then a partial view of a friendly face, came as company to a name, all buried at that end of Riverside.

He carried a flashlight in one hand, the beam shut off, as he started down the middle road in the black of night. It was close to one o'clock, a small disturbance puffed about in the air as if a flock of birds had lifted off into the night sky, and the new stretch of music clearly came to him from the heart of something other than darkness. He could feel it, not an immense declaration, but nevertheless a subtle incision into his psyche.

A hurried listing of adjectives swam upward within him as the music stretched itself in long reach. Things moving at him were nostalgic, moody, real, even before he heard the commencing words of a song he'd not heard before, not that he

12

was any great aficionado of music. *Halleluiah* crawled to his ears out of a far crater, cavern, cave, moving within itself and echoing at the same time… making its own space…demanding space… *Ha… lay… loo… yah… Ha… lay… loo… yah… Ha… laaay… loooo… yaaaaah.* It was not a church song, as something else was vibrating in it, a touching, a reaching, a contemplative self-searching soul at its own observation and lamentation.

The duty sergeant halted in his steps as the small piece of the music hung over him and then dove into his own soul. *Ha… laaaay… loooo… yaaaaahhhh.* The sense coming at him was *plaintive,* he said within. For the moment he could find no other word to carry his feelings.

And then *wondrous,* he thought, some out-of-this-world element clutching at him, or leaping up from his innermost person as the haunting but sparse words made the deepest impression on him he could imagine. It was indeed making itself memorable and he was aware of the impact; haunting, sparse, riveting, grabbing him, stopping him in his tracks there on the middle road, forcing him to listen, to attend.

Plaintive, he said again, and *pensive.* Again, *wondrous.*

In a wild moment of self analysis, he could not decide if the song rose up through his body or fell on him, grabbed him or stabbed him, touched his own reservoir of being or passed cleanly through his body and his senses and went elsewhere, perhaps like an x-ray, full of mystery but producing its mission, or the idea of electricity itself moving magic on wires without resistance. The mood created was greater than any magic he might have known. The darkness, he thought, might have a great deal to do with the impact, and the singer being unknown to him, singing in that darkness deeper than black was meant to be.

And right in the midst of that magic and measurement, life, in all its vagaries, its quick twists and turns, took entry. There came the strident, acidic yells of an angry man, who Culberson figured must be old man Grafton come down from his Mount Sinai, otherwise known as Henshit Mountain, screaming his own midnight disturbance at the unknown singer, guitarist, musician, magician. "Hey, you son of a bitch, I called the cops on you for

13

disturbing the peace, and if they aren't going to do something about you, I goddamn will!"

Those words gave Culberson the impression that a two by four or a baseball bat was being waved as wand of threat. Even as he began to run toward the singer, he tried to picture what Grafton looked like, having seen him a few times at Town Meeting making other wild demands. Nothing came to him but a Teddy Williams swing at the plate, slightly upper-cutting in its swing, demonstrative in its aim.

He ran faster, the flashlight suddenly stabbing a small tunnel of light ahead of him on the pavement of the road, bouncing on stone faces, names he could not read.

It appeared to Culberson that Grafton was about as far from the singer as he himself was, his voice coming from on high, probably from just inside the stone wall that lined the cemetery on Winter Street and ran the whole length of Riverside. In his mind's eye he could even see the bronze marker in the sidewalk noting the walk was laid by the WPA in the depressed '30s.

In those few moments, all the magic disappeared, the lamentation, the mystery, the internal glory that had warmed Culberson warmer than he had been in a long time. Downhill went the mood, the coveted tones, the music of the plucked and strummed strings. Reality came like a curtain closing down on a great Broadway show's final performance.

"It's about goddamned time someone from the police got here. I called it seems forever ago. This crap, this midnight sneaking about, has been going on for too long and I, for one, am damned sick and tired of it." His arms stabbed the air, semaphoring.

Culberson flashed the light on the singer, then on the screamer off the hill. Here they are, he thought, and here I am, right smack in the middle. It was like being between heaven and hell, for the music still flavored him, clung at him, and Sewell Grafton was yet screaming and cursing at the musician, now standing open-mouthed but song-less against the shining granite slabbed mausoleum, his guitar hanging by his side. His thin and pale face, as if nutrition had been a recent problem, cut at the sergeant, tossed his mind back onto a few highlight photos of

14

other singers as though they were looking for the next meal and needing it. He also noted the guitar case was completely opposite in condition from the instrument itself, a reflection of a distant light source coming off its wooden surface.

"He's not hurting you," Culberson said. "The kid's pretty good with that guitar, plays real well. You want me to throw him in jail just to shut up some good music? That song he was playing is damned special. I never heard it before, but I know I'll hear it again. If you are any way attentive to what's going on around us, you'll hear it too. That's a promise I'll make for the kid." He paused for breath, thinking Sewell was going to leap down his throat, but saw, in the eyes lit by the flashlight, that the crank was at a pause. "Get on home now, Mr. Sewell. I'll take care of the youngster. You're making more noise than he did. I'm sure some of your neighbors haven't appreciated that. Go on now, go home. SPD has responded to your call. Please go, sir, before there is a confrontation that needs not to happen."

The next night, Riverside Cemetery, at the far end from the Center, against the small stream working its waters to the Father of Oceans a bare five miles away, was infiltrated by at least one hundred people, mostly young, extremely subdued, quiet, patient, at just past the hour of midnight. All had heard about the night before, about the guitar player and singer, about the noisy crank off Henshit Mountain, about the police sergeant's claim that he had been transfixed, his whole being, by one song, one voice, for mere moments. They had come to hear, to believe, to place a value on something new. Hoping for it, looking for it, for a matrix of a new music or a new voice. Losing sleep would be worth it, or being late for work in the morning. To some a special song was important, or a new voice to capture and captivate. Before last night, it was apparent, nobody had heard of young Cavin Woodmarsh.

The night was hot and starless and Culberson's T-shirt was tacky underarm. Out of uniform, on the other side of the stream running beside the cemetery and along the old and unused B&M railroad tracks, in a pal's back yard on Auburn Court, Culberson and his pal were sharing the moment and a few cold beers. Occasional lights, mayhap cigarette lighters or match flares, gave evidence of the crowd, gathered in hushed testimony, their conduct unimpeachable. Culberson believed he understood why they had come.

"You tell me what you think, Hal, you have a better ear for music than me, that is, if the kid shows up at all. I might have my doubts."

"It figures," Hal said, a member of the local fire department and on the inside of all town events from whatever perspective, "that the crank from the hill has exerted some influence, but he sure hasn't bothered that gang of kids over there now, though I know Nora Furbish and her husband Harry are in the mix. They walked down the Court to get there, talking about it as they passed by, and walked all around the Center end of the cemetery to get there. That means they're interested, if only curious. But we don't know. They're on the edge of one element of age, like you said about the in-betweeners and how they're either joining or leaving one or the other no matter what gear they're in."

"I didn't think you'd remember that little talk of ours, Hal. And speaking about Nora, she's always been an absolute knockout and therefore always in the mix of talk and such."

Hal snickered. "You mean dreams count too?"

"With her, absolutely. Always has. Saw her once off a diving board, bare-ass ballicky and have never forgotten the sight. Seems a hundred years ago. Dreams count and with this new kid plunker over there too. I think he's coming now." He strained to look off into the heart of the cemetery, locking his eyes on small pieces of light falling upon those who had gathered. "Jeezus, Hal, that gang of kids is parting for him like the water parted for Moses. That spells more than curiosity, a kind of respect all rolled into one ball."

Hal stared too, finding a fleck of amazement coming at him in concert. "How'd you get old crank Sewell off the kid's back, and yours too?"

"Told him if he found himself running counter to something brand new and good, he was going to look awfully bad on that council seat he's holding, getting free summer camp for some kids that couldn't get it otherwise. Told him this new kid

16

could be so connected to that kind of stuff without half trying that it'd be a shame to wreck a great opportunity." He held a thought for a minor second and continued, "It's as though he only operates or reacts to threat or fear."

"Nuff said for me," Hal responded, knocking off another beer, tipping the bottle to his pal in a sum of agreement.

Cavin Woodmarsh, about a half hour past midnight, plunked a single note on the guitar and the single note slipped into the night like a tonal comet. Instantly the dark audience was still, sitting on grass or stones, standing at total attention as if a maestro at the Pops or Symphony Hall had flicked his baton. Culberson and his pal stood rigid in Hal's back yard, no more than one hundred and fifty feet from the granite mausoleum and the originator of the one note. Both realized they were transfixed, believed they were about to hear new magic come from the young man who had gathered the crowd in darkness, at the end of the cemetery, in a starless but warm night. Moisture sat in abeyance, and mystery, and motion ... and all other sound, from every quarter of Saugus and the universe, kept its distance.

When Culberson stared into the darkness it deepened and everything –the gathering of music lovers, the mood of the night, the mood of the town, the mood of two old pals standing in a piece of that darkness – became part of night's tone. Something, Culberson said to himself, was reaching for everything the senses knew, the taste of rain, the smell of grass cut that day, the glittering quasi stars almost at eye level, the phantom hands reaching to touch and make a universal connection, the echo of the first note. The lit ends of a few cigarettes showed how well they could replace the stars long hidden by thick clouds promising showers in the hot night, as if a matter of combustion waited its peril.

From the façade of the mausoleum, like shivering tonal work at Symphony Hall, or clear as a Mass bell at Matins, a second note rose and covered distance so rapidly one had to hold it immediately to memory or hold what it had caused or created within the mind, heart, or soul, as it fled through and past. It was an extension of the first note still holding sway, not all gone away to ether.

Rigid attention asserted itself as broad as the dark night, breaths held, belief taking place.

"Jesus, God," Hal said and put a half bottle of beer back on the picnic table. "This kid is more than mystery. I bet I heard some of those notes the last few nights and I thought I was dreaming.

Oh, the dreams we think and talk about. I recognize those notes. Dear God." A dear, dear night, he thought, was about to come upon them.

It was then that stupid, noisy, cranky, inconsonant Sewell Grafton, unable to change his stance in spite of Sgt. Culberson's prior and veiled threat to his reputation, once again threatened to destroy some beautiful thing as he yelled out, "No more of that frigging crap, mister. I'll call the cops again. I'll get them here pronto." He spread his arms about, to encompass the gathering. "For all of you." He started to move forward in the darkness, bare bulbs of streetlights soft as false dawn touching along the base of the hill. He had penetrated the edge of the gathering, knowing he was in the wide plot of the Stockman family, which had an early and steady impact on the town, had once owned the entire hill he lived on.

Disgraceful.

Grafton's activities, as well as Cavin Woodmarsh's, had obviously made the rounds of town. A flutter of noise rose in the cemetery, a very minor disturbance, casual almost, and Sewell Grafton spoke no more. Two very strong young men sat him down between them on the grass of Harland Stockman's grave. In the flash of a cigarette lighter the engraving would have read *Harland Stockman 1890 – 1981* and *Helen Stockman 1899 -* . And Helen herself might still be clinging to life, perhaps on the road above the cemetery, or nearby, another of the old breed on for a new ride. The young men were also from Henshit Mountain.

One of them, in the darkness said, "I am not threatening you, mister, but I am telling you to keep quiet, listen, and I swear that tonight you will be converted from the hell that has been your life."

"You've got no right to do this to me, like that singer has no right to sing at this time of night."

18

"Don't be stupid, Mr. Grafton. Look around you. See the crowd. You'd recognize a lot of faces, people you've known or at least been aware of for a long time."

"I don't need to be curried by you and a crowd of Hippies. I speak my own mind. You can't take that away from me."

"I can do that very easily, Mr. Grafton."

"How?"

"By telling people, including you, what your wife had to say about you the day she died. With her last breath, sir, her last breath. I could yell it out now so the whole town would know, not just a few of us off Henshit Mountain."

Sewell Grafton, seeing his life spinning before him in a dizzying approach, carrying everything with it... the dread moments of meanness, the harnessed cruelty that had blossomed in him on too many occasions, the touch of flesh his hands and knuckles distinctly remembered, sat down atop Harland Stockman's final home, as though he had fainted. The heat touched his face, came up through his buttocks, and there was a momentary acceptance of Hell at hand.

And, in the assured silence, in the heavy heat and the heavy darkness, off the façade of the granite mausoleum in some perfection of acoustic clarity, came the voice of the tall, lean young singer with the midnight voice many singers yearn and covet for years on end, for full lifetimes.

Halleluiah, he let free, *Haaa laaaay looo yaaah.* Nobody in the large gathering breathed for long moments, open-mouthed though, waiting more, absorbing what had come at them, *Haaa laaaay looo yaaah.*, the tone of it, the reach of it, the grace of it, the sincere and soaring clarity of his voice and the words, be they words or inner expressions of a thousand granite or marble stone faces and the utter and total acceptance the cemetery carried from that moment on.

Some people there that night, in later days, telling of the experience, said, "Cavin started at the back end of the song and brought us up to creation, back to front, up to creation itself, took us to the beginning, his beginning, and we were knowing it at the same moment. We lived his dream, and we ushered him into the world."

19

Amen, they could have said: "We knew we had to share him, from that moment on."

Man in a Pinch

He was thinking if he had a deep jacket pocket he would thrust his right hand into that pocket, hide it. But of course, he couldn't. That right hand was laying back there on the rock, near the stump of the tree that had fallen back on him, pinned his hand on the rock.

All on his own, he had come this far. He was in the forest alone, his best pal and fellow woodsman Eddie gone south a long time now, and the blood was still pooling in his lap... a mass of blood, from that arm without a hand, that arm without a wrist.

Ginger would surely throw his jeans in the garbage pail.

He remembered the first time, on a camping trip thirty or more years earlier, Eddie had said, "Between a rock and a hard place." Now he knew. Before it had been a reach of words, a mere expression; now it was hard fact.

Left handed, leaning and twisting his frame, awkward with virulent pain talking trash talk to him, he turned the key in the Jeep ignition and heard the engine cough into life. Of all things, he was thinking about payback. The constant oil changes were paying off, those seemingly casual gestures at maintenance that in themselves could hold a whole life together for the long run, if you could hang on for the long run.

His feet played with clutch and gas pedal, measured torque and searing pain in the same breath. Looking down into his lap, at that mess, he didn't know how long he would last. How much was unthinkable, imaginable? In through the steering wheel he reached again, stretching, daring, like a gymnast in a weird exercise, somebody watching and nobody watching, and shifted into second gear. The sounds of doubt rose, personified, striking like the heart of a bell, shaking his whole being. He thought about crawling through life... inhaling lead paint residue, breathing it, stuffing his lungs with it, tasting it, life in the slow lane.

His mind wandered again. Found pain. Came back.

The Jeep transmission ground as if he hadn't guided the splines at the correct entry. He heard metallic misery. The pains he knew, there was more than one of them, coming from more than one source, were ripping through him. Ginger and Paulie came as vague light reflections on the surface of the windshield. No way could he tell if they were on the outside of the glass or on the inside. His kin. Her skin. Oh, her skin was as pink and as keen as ever, the clear shine yet evident, still broadcasting the life within. How rich she was in body. How she could mesmerize him. Once he had told her she was lucent and rutilant and she had smiled an acceptance at the unknown words, trusting his mind in all the matter of words. How was he so damn lucky? She was in the rearview mirror too. Ever present Ginger. Oh, God, he'd miss her and Paulie like he all ready missed his right hand, half his forearm. How had he done it? If he had hit the stop bar on the chain saw, it would have shut off immediately. Was he that lucky? Or unlucky. He had come this far. How far could he go? Perhaps to the main road would carry it off.

The wheels slipped on the edge of the rough road, branches slapping at him and the windshield, riding on the fenders and the hood, trying to hit him. Darkness and dimness came in quick little shifts of light, and vagueness and peril. If the engine ever quit on him, it would be over and done with. Up ahead there was the lingering promise of a fork in the road. There *was* a fork in the road. Only one turn would get him to the main road, perhaps some traffic, perhaps an observant driver, perhaps an off-duty EMT or a fireman. Maybe a nurse. He could only pray for a doctor, perhaps a day-off doctor with a fishing rod in the back seat, a creel heavy with supper's trout, a rainbow filling the creel with dreamed promise, one hook still imbedded in his jaw.

The other way at the fork ended nowhere but at the impassable stream. He tried to think of the left turn and the right turn. Was the right turn the right turn? Was left right or right right? Why all these mental games when the blood was still pooling? Brightest red and still pooling. "In the trash with them," Ginger would say, pointing out the back door, her skin shiny, her hair flame red, her lips full of promise. Paulie'd see everything with his big blue eyes.

And the voices, of course, were evaluating his foray into the deep woods… alone.

The last night, before going off to Florida for good, Eddie had said, "Now hear this. This is the captain speaking. Do not go gentle into the good woods alone. Never alone. We made that rule a dozen years ago. It still holds true. Even if I have to go away, get me to the new job, move five kids over half the country, do not go gentle into those good woods." Of course, he was playing Dylan Thomas games with him, this non-poetic friend. He said it again, "Do not go gentle into those good woods." He did not know Eddie had studied that poem, though he knew every line from Gilbert and Sullivan. Poems were anathema to him, except his poems, the few he showed to Eddie. But it was Eddie's way... he had struck out on his own, reached for poetry, or a little sense of it. Had come away with the gentle warning... Do not go gentle into those good woods, into that deep forest. Not alone.

The single ash tree, like an icon in the forest on his last walk through with the dog, had called at him again and again. Their kind was leaving fast, fading into the mulch of the forest and few of them growing. The excessive demand for charcoal had cut their lifeline. This one tree hung on the edge of a flat hearth of a rock, an expanse of many square yards, a blue granite giving off hard promise. The tree kept saying, "I am yours. I am yours."

For the life of him he could not remember the last time he had seen an ash tree, and when this one went bad, almost overnight, like some new disease had raped it repeatedly, he had made up his mind to cut it down and bring it home, burn it on Saturday nights, good company for a hockey game, a six pack of beer, a few moments of silence and deep blue flame in the mix of fire. It would be a celebration. He'd tell Eddie about it, masquerading the fact of his lone entry into the woods, the Husqvarna chain saw at his side. It was a horse of a chain saw, and would chew up a Sequoia if needed.

But this last ash tree treated him as a novice, its unusual grotesque trunk twisting the wrong way, falling the wrong way, pinning his arm on top of the large flat slab of blue granite catching at the sun. It would take dynamite to move it. Or a wad of C3 in the right package, like a fuse lies in waiting for a strike to take place in a bowling alley... everything asunder and then some. Fitzhugh from old years came back in his mind, with nasty plastic C3 loads digging foxholes for everybody in the company in Korea in the dead of winter. Until one blast blew off the back of his head.

23

Good old Fitzhugh. Good gone Fitzhugh. He should have been a safecracker; he was so good with the stuff, until the Big Bang. One time he voiced that dream to easy riches, being a yeggman, *Second Story Specialist 3.* He made everybody laugh, except for the last time.

He was not sure when he realized he could not extract his hand, the end of his arm. It was pinned by a ton of wood trunk, mean as all hell. The blue granite rock had a grip never known, not in these woods. Nobody knew where he was, stupid him, wanting to bring home a surprise for a night out in front of the fireplace. God no. Eddie had said, "Do not go gentle into those good woods," and here he was pinned down, perhaps for eternity.

The ash tree had spun on him in its fall, the weight of limbs higher than he thought, throwing top weight about like a wrestler, and a curse of a hold and a curse of a throw. He had tried to escape the roll, but a mere piece of bark, crude in shape, ugly by nature, had grasped at his sweater. It took him in. He twisted away and was hooked in by recoil of his own body. He was knocked down by the swinging of the trunk. It fell on his hand. It pinned his hand to the blue granite... his hand and much of his right arm.

The Husqvarna was still purring its pretty song as it lay beside him. Pretty song. Constant song. Could do a Sequoia if needed. Animal sounds rode on a slight breeze coming in from the northwest with a chill, and everything dangerous after a fashion... the coming night, the cold weather promised as ever in early October, toothy critters of various sorts, loss of blood, unconsciousness a promise if the status stayed quo. *Darkness* sounded its voice, then *dread*, then *death.*

He saw the dark headline, the black ribbons of it... *Fatal fall.* The smell of newsprint came back from wherever. It shook itself loose in his mind. He wondered what else what else was loose in his body... life running loose?

Reality came back: no matter how hard he tried, or how subtly, as if not breathing in each attempt, sneaking up on freedom, he could not move his hand, never mind extracting it. Shock had him in a grip, he was positive. For the moment there was little pain. But it would come. That was a promise.

Other thoughts began to crowd him. Ginger came and went away; the shine fell away with the lost image. He was aware he could never wield the saw long enough or at a proper angle to cut through the trunk of the tree. The gas might last a half hour in the tank of the saw, purring pretty in its song, pretty pretty song. He loved the hum of it and thought of all the hours he had worked on it, keeping it primed and ready; hours on end, humming, humming, tune of his existence, labor his due in life.

Observations came to mind: no other tools were at hand. The Jeep was thirty yards away, his tool box setting on the rear seat, the trailer clean of logs, life at a fulcrum, a bend one way or the other and it was complete for him.

There was only one out for him. His belt, with difficulty, came loose of the loops in his jeans, and he managed to place it, with more difficulty, around his right arm. It was drawn snug, and then tightened around the arm above the elbow. As expected, as if he had known all along, the pain began in earnest, long series of jolts and jabs that rang in his brain loud as bells or sirens. Whenever lightning might hit him broadside from above, he swore he would know it.

But for now, there was no other way out of it. He prayed all his keen and persevering maintenance would prove itself, as he shifted the Husqvarna into position, held it over his own wrist, squeezed the trigger, raced that purring beauty into a high dance of danger and dropped it onto his wrist. He dared not pass out. The bones, the sheer, thin bones of that arm shattered under the impact. The teeth of that ugly son of a bitch tore through skin and bone. Those teeth rapped like lightning on the rock face. Threw hundreds of sparks into the air. Clattered into silence.

He left his hand behind. He crawled away and left his hand behind, and part of his arm. And his ugly Husqvarna chain saw. The ugly red saw! Clumsily, he crawled a dozen feet at first, away from the rock, toward freedom, toward the Jeep. His keys luckily were still in the ignition. If they had been in his pocket, in the right side pocket of his jeans, he'd have to drop his pants to get the keys.

The engine turned over. Glory for working gear, he thought, for good oil, for true maintenance. Testing the horn, he blasted it and blasted it again, and again, as if the lonely blare, the raucous blare, would drown out elements of his pain, a shred of pain, a shard of pain, any piece of his pain. Now, in earnest, with the remnants of sanity and judgment, he began to measure his endurance and condition, his whereabouts. The whole lottery of his chances.

The Jeep responded to his stubborn left hand, his knees guiding the steering wheel at some point, and the blood still pooling up in his lap. Images leaped at him for grasping. He pictured his mother at her knitting or darning, the needles at work, her lap a collection of all kinds of sewing gear. The kitchen was so small, the fireplace so big, she might have been inconspicuous. Once there was a blue apron with smiling monkeys on it. Blue monkeys. He remembered the blue monkeys. For a fraction of a second, he saw her face, and then she went off with Ginger, off with Paulie, to where blackness seemed to be resurrecting itself.

The rugged Jeep crawled at his commands, along the road, beside the log he had moved on his way in rather than maneuvering around it. Fortunate planning. A turn right was the right turn, he was sure, and found the steep banking he'd have to climb to get up on the paved road. He needed to be on the road and prayed no one would run into the side of the Jeep. Soon it would be dark. Too soon it would be too cold for him. If he got onto the road, he'd have to pray for traffic.

The accelerator responded to his foot, and in first gear that was difficult to find with his left hand, he climbed up the sharp incline and grounded the Jeep on the crown of the road. The engine shut down abruptly, shaking the carriage of the vehicle, shaking his arm. Pain shot into his brain. Passed into his brain from that lost hand, the lost wrist, that portion of an arm. The trailer was exerting a torque on the Jeep, trying to hold it back, draw it back down the incline. At a point of balance, at a fulcrum wedge under his life, Ginger and Paulie on one side of the road, him on the backside of survival, came light and noise in stiff argument.

In his head lights faded in and out. The sound of the horn beat in his ears. He could feel the light going away at the back of his head. He knew he would be cold. Ginger's face was looking at him, shining in the fading light. He heard Eddie saying, "Do not go gentle into that good wood."

That other horn, that other alarm, was diesel in nature.

The Emergence of Slow Purple

Here I was, forty-five years later, coming back to Saugus, looking to find something I had lost. Though I'd been told I was still considered somewhat quasi-handsome for my age, a place in the world carved by my love of and for tools, enfranchised in a hardware business that offered heady spoils and wealth beyond first dreams, I felt hollow. Empty. Concave. I didn't know what my loss was; I could bring no tool to measure it, me, the master of tools, helpless, exposed at last.

My wife Cricket, dead for these long and lonely 15 years, had gradually receded but never really left me. She would not allow herself to leave all at once when she died, for there was so much to hang onto. But the separation grew, lengthened, managed to steal some of me, then lots of me. The hollowness came in tow, like nothing follows nothing. Air stretching a balloon. The fabric of an idea. My Cricket on the move, a thermal as tiny as an idea.

The fishing plagued me with perplexity, nagged at me as I looked down at my old hometown from a window seat on the plane. The shape or force of that perplexity had earlier come with a full-bodied question mark, feeling it was worn outright and visible on my person… a costume complete with epaulets, chevrons, insignia, all parts of it. Times came when I swore I could feel the drape of that costume settling on my frame.

Below our flight path I saw the spread of the Rumney Marsh, the blast north of Route 1 as it blew out of Boston, the hills I ran free on as a kid. On Baker Hill the standpipe was gone, houses crowded themselves in realtor fashion. I remembered blueberry patches on the slopes.

For some time I had accepted a number of things about myself. One of the acceptances came often, stayed longest, dug deepest: *loneliness,* it said, *comes with silence, darkness, a cold river, a thick forest, anyplace at odds with activity or brightness or a day running with itself.* I had been through all those elements, whatever the name presented or image given, and was coming home, I hoped, to escape the loneliness shrouding me, my soul beleaguered. Discomfort is a strange bedfellow.

Yet I had a slim hope, home. In promise, the plane dipped its nose off the horizon.

Some decent friends say I appear pleasant enough in a rugged, individual way; a face chiseled a bit by time, chosen of a good lot, hair dark and full, but eyes perhaps not saying what I am thinking, not read of them. Those eyes, in fact, might have made me a stick-out on this trip. While I wore a dark and neat blue blazer and a light blue shirt without a tie, my pants were rugged jeans atop rugged boots. In some other light I could have been a contradiction, or in some circles. A small mole, perched on my right ear lobe, appears as an almost decorative but dark earring, catching the inquisitive eye immediately, a wandering eye almost as soon.

Loneliness is a place. I went *there* again, in my search. And came up again with a void.

How long I had been aware of the nature of the void, I could no longer remember. At times I accepted it as my shadow acting out at high noon… in me, with me, but unseen in the vertical existence. Back behind an indistinct form or structure were a scattering of stray moments of my early life; not many, but enough to hang onto. Apparently a few of those moments had swept me up, sent me on this journey.

As the plane nosed into a long curve at approach, the sun screamed on the horizon as though it were yelling out the name of the town, but all I heard in that swift separation of sun from horizon was "home."

Images from the past flew at me and reflections rose as the plane tipped lower; I swore I could touch some of the images, even in their quick rush. I went backwards in thought.

Schoolmates and pals had called me "Tools" from about my seventh year. The decision of name-setting had been easy; at play after school I continually walked around with a leather tool belt slung on my hips the way other kids might wear a cowboy gun belt. Every day I ran home from school to don my belt, snug it tightly in place, check the belt's components. I never said *bang* at a pistol or revolver shot, but at the proper burial of a nail by a hammer in one unerring smash. The belt and the nickname, like character development, fit me in a pivotal way. Later on they said

29

I had the appropriate hands, and the eye, and knew all the theory of mechanics and its classic relatives. Thus, the name stuck with me all the way through adulthood, the way a scar hangs on, at times a neat diversion, at times nothing more than a jaunty embarrassment.

The flight today had been serene, though I had slept fitfully for an hour or so at one stretch. Now, in the baggage claim area at the airport, at the end of a row of seats, I rested my bothersome knee. All my life, away from this city, I'd been a people watcher, and at this break I studied those in transition about me, the fellow travelers, the lost now homeward bound, the celebrators, the newly wearied with the foreign look in their eyes, and slack set on their chins. I marked a turbaned man, a young man in military uniform, a pair of lovers so engrossed they saw nobody else, and nobody knew if they were coming or going.

I always wondered about *their* stories.

My eyes, random at first in their search, settled at length on a stately gentleman and a very neat and tall female companion dressed in casual gray slacks, a pale green sweater and earrings I had not seen before; gentle travel wear, comfortable but without obvious style. Once, I was sure, she had been a radiant blonde. The combination of the couple attracted me, the woman at first athletic and graceful in movement; the man slower, searching for steps. Their hands were alert for each other's.

Something of the woman's youth remained in place at her hips; slimness, perhaps grace, practice at good health, weight management, activity. The display was subtle but legible, a combination speaking about confidence, surety, need. The couple to me was real; in them I could feel some kind of energy on the move. The woman's facial light, her shine, said she was a care giver, deeply invested in a current case; her hand not letting go of her companion's hand all the while. Not for a second had she let go of his hand since I had first spotted them coming down the concourse, her partially elegant, him partially unsure of some of the surroundings, each step of his worried, measured, practiced.

The intrigue, and the curiosity, crept through me as sure as welcome warmth. I loved the supposition of goodness in all such subjects, especially at airports and railroad stations. In my time,

I'd been at a thousand places, seen a thousand travelers, I supposed myself keen at their make-up.

A word unnerved itself from my vocabulary, broke loose, said *devotion;* as if I had sent for it, the word coming across the air like a small pennant waving for attention, touching at my mind-set, bringing images. I had seen the same coupling at a few nursing homes when visiting two long-time employees at the last edges of life. This wasn't all new to me.

Then, a voice, barely intrusive, mellow, with a built-in *pardon* hanging in place, came from a man sitting a seat away from me. "I spotted them too, but her first," the voice said, and quickly added, "Some days I sit here half a day just looking at people in their passage, wondering where they've been, where they're going. I thought at the outset you were a people watcher too. Saw it in your eyes, the interest, and," he paused again, "in your facial expression. You care for strangers, or have deep wonder."

There was no embarrassment in his words, at his intrusion. "You spotted that in her, didn't you? The simplicity that generates life, then holds on for whatever comes along with it. What we'd call a keeper keeping up, like the marriage vows unfolding all the way open." It might have been a sermon I was hearing.

I turned my full attention to the source of the voice. It had come from a quickly pleasant man with a wide forehead cut short by thick black hair perhaps colored for effect. The hair seemed to be too dark to be the real thing. There were contradictions. Somewhere in this stranger's past there had been a confrontation, a fight, a meeting with a hard object, for his nose was marked by harsh encounter. But it was marked in a rather insignia way; the man was a survivor of something. And the face was an old and worn face, the eyes older and then some, but at home for a late turn at comfort, for ease, as if patience bore well or wore well with him.

Assessing him as a long-retired teacher or professor with years in front of students, I guessed him comfortable with words, saying them with venerated practice, moving gracefully with chosen words around a classroom, his stature evident, measurable, his footsteps nearly silent. No other evidence of age or infirmity loomed visible, though he was well into his 80s; no cane or crutch, no dropped or discounted lip or droopy eye, no slur in the voice, no hand cursed by a half-grotesque knot and held helpless at his side. Hale he was, and apparently in one good and decent piece.

A quick plunge of favor found its way in me, a sudden warmth, a catch at an inner spirit of joy. I believed that I liked the stranger without knowing any more about him, as though, in some measure, he would count, would matter. If the sun had popped up on a dark horizon, I would have felt the same way.

Nodding agreement, studying with interest the nose of the man with interests, I said, "You are correct on that point, sir. She bears the care of a nurse, the grace of a lover, the patience of a mother. You, I assume, nameless to me at this point, agree."

"Yes, I do. On all points. Oh, they call me 'Rags,' sir. And that's just about everybody I know. They've done so for years, for things I did as a youngster. Believe it, I was an early recycler of useable goods… cloth, newspapers and magazines, aluminum pots and pans, copper and lead, anything the junkman would buy from ten cents a pound up to the really good stuff, like copper, mercury, enough scrap lead for tin soldiers by the thousands, armies of them." I saw the imagery in his eyes. "But mostly my payment came from old clothes, worn clothing, so I was 'Rags' to one and all."

Heartily, still warmer in my appreciation, I started to laugh. I held out my hand to the old man, the new acquaintance. "Rags," I said, "meet Tools." Two men of this world laughed easily, in an unconscious way, provoked a bit but totally reactive. We laughed loud and long, so long that the stately couple had disappeared, apparently gone off into life, while my suitcase still floated on the luggage console, the final piece to be claimed. People along the concourse eyed the two of us; some smiled at the noisy gaiety, some merely nodded with understanding.

"What brings you here?" Rags said, standing beside me as I grabbed my single suitcase from the console. Rags seemed nimble enough, getting to the console as soon as I did, knee and all. His khaki pants, government-issue color, were pressed with distinct iron edges down the seams, and his checkered shirt, open at the collar, exposed no chest hair. The belt cinching Rags' waist had no sudden bloat to its circumference. A quick shine came from his shoe tops, and I registered *care, neatness and preservation* for the man. A sudden sense of synesthesia, in my growing awareness, came on me. I welcomed it like a gift.

"You been here before?" Rags said. "Coming for a reunion? I tried to figure out what you were doing here, besides watching people like I do. I'm not prying, but observing; it's a way of life with me and will end in my journal, if you will permit me. Saw you come in earlier, the limp evident, the quick seat you took for that reason. I'd rather sit here than in a bar with a cool one, though I've enjoyed that fare too." He nodded a distant assent.

Rags answered his own question, shook his head, smiled, and said, "If you're going off to Saugus or near there, I'd ride out that way with you if you have the wheels. I live there, about 12 miles out from here. I don't drive anymore, or I don't keep a car. Too damn expensive for me. I hustle rides, if you can believe it. I'm really a ride hustler. I love this airport, the comings and goings, new faces or old friends." He facially measured his last statement, and then appended, "Though there's damn few of them these days." Came then a throaty assessment of self agreement, a small cough, almost a word. He would bear some understanding, I knew.

I nodded my answer first, then vocalized it. "One hustler to another... I am going to Saugus. I have a rental waiting on me here, down the line somewhere. But the trouble is, I really don't know why I've come back. Come home, in a manner of speaking. I grew up in Saugus and left the day after high school graduation. I've never been back. The whole journey feels like it began yesterday, though, or, perhaps, late last night."

Rags recognized my whole bit of facial punctuation as a question mark.

Wearing the look of another new care giver, Rags said he was still curious. He wore an aura I could feel the way one senses a source of heat in the darkness, a sterling emanation.

"I love a mystery, that's for damn sure," he said. "It leads me to say you have a haunt working on you, an old face, a kiss you can't forget and can't remember, at least not all the way? You

33

wear a tunnel in your eyes, yea, a pair of tunnels. I haven't seen that look in a long time. It's the way a person might look at a house he used to live in, and can suddenly feel the rooms collide inside himself, the noise coming back, the faces almost gone but hanging on for the catch of a memory, somebody long gone but back for an instant." He held up both hands in a sign of halting, as if he had proceeded too far too quickly.

"You're right there on the mark, Rags," I said. "Will that go in your journal… a man found, a look at, a discovery or revelation? I'm not sure what brings me back. I keep looking for a good concrete reason and can't find one. All my old pals, such as they were, have moved on one way or another. I bet I haven't heard from a single one of them in 20 or 30 years. Could be more if I was a counter all the time. But I lost my wife about 15 years ago, after a damn good marriage. We had no kids and she let me get buried in my work when I needed it. That's where I really took myself when Cricket died, deeper into the work. Been there ever since."

The smile when I pronounced her name came warm and sincere. "Something brought me out of it. Perhaps it's only the promise of a small adventure. It might be the river here, upstream on a cool morning, or a breeze coming across the marsh, carrying something in the air, sending something."

My pause was a dominant punctuation. "Whatever," I said, as if in partial measurement, "it got me here."

Rags shifted about on one leg, searching out balance, found it. "Cricket? Like a little chirper? A cute little trick with lots of energy? You give her that name, Tools?"

Rags asked questions, I thought, that made his approach warm, the way he framed them, softening an otherwise harsh impact, gaining ground on his own. Rags had quickly changed the direction of the conversation. I took him by the arm, and nodded toward the car rental counter.

He continued. "You know there's not much to pick from room-wise in Saugus, if you want to get away from the real commercial stuff, away from the Pike. I have a pal who has a furnished rental available. I get a cut if I land it for her, as long as

I do my one chore a day on the place. It's not too expensive either, but you have to take it for a month anyway."

"You're the Saugus Welcome Wagon, Rags. We'll take a look." Much further down the concourse, and through a wide window, I saw the tall care giver woman in the green sweater and the gray slacks guide her companion into a taxi. She placed her hand on top of his head the way a policeman does it. With a silent praise I saluted her.

"And you have to tell me about *one chore a day*."

Retrieving the rental car, we two new friends, and old strangers, set out for Saugus, Rags noting quickly the easy and comfortable driving skills I possessed on the circuitous drive out of the airport proper. "On more than one occasion," he admitted, "I've ridden with a driver who had made a wrong turn and headed back into Boston. Took the new tunnel to get lost."

I said, "Tell me about this *one chore a day* and who's the party that established it. Makes me think it's a pretty sound concept. One chore a day, in a month, can get a lot done, never mind a whole year." I thought over the options and added, "As long as some of the chores have teeth in them, make demands on the person doing the chores."

The traffic was thinning alongside us we came across the Marsh Road, the Saugus sign a solid black on gray cast iron announcing its perimeter on the saline and brackish spread of the Rumney Marsh. Rags slowly turned in his seat. "You are perceptive, my man, very perceptive. She's a niece of mine, though at some distance. Inherited the house from within the family. It's no great place, modest in fact, and needs a ton of work, but it's cheap enough for her to handle as long as I do my one chore a day and try to keep down extra maintenance costs." His pause was selfless. "For what that's worth." He laughed again showing a hand marked with a few harsh knuckles.

That exposed edge of his thought I caught. "You're saying she has more motive in her madness, Rags? She has a plan? She thinks ahead? Sounds like a helluva woman. What's your take on her?"

"Let's face it, Tools. I've seen the raw edges of life, day and night. Felt them too, day and night. All the raw edges. No place not seen. No deed not done. Not on my road everywhere and nowhere. All over the world, being my own enemy, as you can imagine. This simple demand on her part is not retribution for my storied past, but it's maintenance at work or maintenance assured. Simple and positive, if you stop to think about it. If she keeps me going, if there's a daily demand, I get some longevity out of it. I get additional life. I get my own kick in the ass. There were times I could have folded it all and laid down, even as recently as a couple of years ago. But she gave me this dictate. An opening. And here I am, moving on, finding things in this life I never knew. Like seeing

that tall lady at the airport taking care of what we assume to be her frail husband. I would never have noticed that before. Mine eyes have seen the glory, I could say." He slapped his knee, let his eyes light up.

"Well," I countered, "I get the picture of her. Or pretty close to what makes her tick. She's certainly understanding. She cares, she loves and she has patience. Now what shape's her house in? As bad as you paint it? And what's her name?"

First he snickered and then laughed loudly and slapped a knee again. "By God, man, you still got the ginger, and we could use a man like you for a month or two. I can see the hammer flashing in your hand, nails getting knocked home in one swing, the skill saw abuzz on the morning air, the crooked fence down and a straight one up. Our own *Habitat for Humanity* on the morning prowl. Get coffee, go to work. A dozen chores a day. A dozen, man!" He laughed loudly and slapped his knee. "I damn well knew this dawning was going to be special!" He chuckled anew, more words buried in his throat. Then, spilling his feeling totally, he shook his fist at the windshield, or at the horizon, or at the blue sky, at whatever.

I decided the fist shake was at the blue sky, a signal, a promise at truth. And I was warmer. I found an old comfort, felt my sort of undernourished body settle into a long-forgotten groove. Knowing myself again. And old movements, old sensations and awareness, were making themselves known deep inside me, like one part of my body talking to another part, telling it how to act, how to get along better. A meter could not have made the parts any more accented; now and then a wire leaped in concert, a loose end in contact with the past, or the future. The possibilities loomed again where they had lain dormant for so long. At least this would bring about a meeting, a confrontation instead of the old daydream of newness. The options, hope said, might be limitless.

"Tell me what she looks like, Rags. How old she is. What's her health like?" I wondered what made me ask that question so hurriedly, trying to clear the decks of worry, and something else trying to take hold, more than plain curiosity. I was back *there* again.

Pictures of Cricket rushed me... her arms thin and getting thinner, her whispering, her stubborn smallness becoming the biggest thing in my life, her slow departure bringing a new rush of agonies never really put aside. Now, on this piece of an old road, she sifted away again, thinner, more shadow, a question rising of where she existed, in what realm.

"Hurry gets you no place, Tools," Rags said. "You know that. Not so fast on the approach, man, though the lady is hale, in her fiftieth year, or close to it." He paused to make a point of it; "I might say it's more or less what a woman makes of the difference. She's inventive as we agreed, and where we think we have something different in *Tools* and *Rags,* she goes by the name of..." His response, a gathering of breath, a shift in his seat as well, was a shift in dramatics, his head turning ever so slightly as he said, half in a pause itself, *"Slow Purple."*

The name, I thought immediately, came with colors attached, a host of them, ablaze in intention, sunlight and moonlight, a bloom in a side yard a whole house lives for, the air filled with a suggestion of simple purple essence, presence of the violet, yet a soft bloom, the coy lavender of it.

I looked at Rags, an inquisitive nod almost taking place at the same time. "Slow Purple?" I mouthed the name a few times, felt it come back in a sweet sensation, the color running at my mouth, the taste of it. A softness flowed with the name. "Slow Purple?" There was a tint on the far horizon, an acuteness I could feel. Without me starting them off, images of her began to take shape.

37

We took a left through an intersection, after a stop sign, before I spoke again. The river ran beside us as we drove and a fleet of lobster boats floated on the high tide, their colors brilliant blue and brilliant red in the slanting sunlight. I felt an old sense of energy and adventure, even as the river and the marsh and the brackish odor pulled me along once more.

"No kidding about that name? That's her real name? It seems to go with the idea of her. I never heard a name like that before. It grabs you. It really does." My eyes were talking too, as if shaken loose from some old post or station of the past. "That's a name to remember," I said.

We rolled up a slight incline, passed through another traffic light, drove by the long curving stone wall of a cemetery. Soon, we passed over idle railroad tracks, went by blocks of stores and through the center of town where a statue and a flagpole stood tall. The traffic and motion were abuzz in the sweet day; townspeople out walking alone or with dogs on leashes, maple limbs hanging in proper disorder, new scents rising in the air. A huge delivery truck double parked on the main street, the engine idling. Two boys on bikes delivered their newspapers, taking turns at houses, flinging papers in a high arc. I thought I heard somebody whistling a tune. It was not Rags.

When we turned the corner, at Rags' direction, the house was directly in front of us. The fence loomed as a first order of business, for it leaned crazily in a snaky way. Then the lack of paint announced itself on just about most surfaces on the front of the house. It was as if the place had been decorated in drear and drab. The porch was half painted, two of the steps were newer than the others, a tall thin flag pole, without rope or flag, had proceeded in many spots to rust.

But there was a distinction about the house, and it was standing out in front of all the need. A shapely woman on the porch facing us was regal, but in a softened way. I parked the rental about twenty feet in front of her; a short walkway of deep gray cement passed through a small patch of good lawn. She was a blonde with mostly interest on her face; eyes, cheekbones, square teeth white as Kilimanjaro, a chin not to push around. There was nothing skimpy about her. Curvy and full-bodied, a mischievous

38

aura was working its way through her presentation. Of course, I knew she was a message center, at her best work, broadcasting herself.

As I looked at her, as she looked down at me with a slight twist to her head, the loose wires in me that had been fumbling around for over a decade made newer connections. Ignition was immediate. There came the near insurmountable old urge to touch myself, to gather all complements, to cup and to measure. It ran through me with its electric charge, its quick vitality. The redness of embarrassment measured me anew. A small gasp caught in my throat. My thighs tightened at the same moment, the sympathetic wires in more connections. Warmth flooded my extremities. I couldn't remember the last time all those muscles had shuddered themselves awake this way. *She* was penetrating *me*.

And she smiled. Slow Purple smiled. It was a new radiance. A blossom.

Standing on her porch steps, not quite as soft as an evening sunset, she was close enough for admiration at that very first glance. Blonde hair swept up on her head, clearly showing blue eyes set fairly apart and a full brow, matched by a tugged-tight blouse and skirt. She didn't need to wear stripes. Another wire touched, flared a spark. Her wave, in spite of the house's cry for more of my attention, was at Rags but her eyes quickly fell on me. I felt a long-gone fever also come at abrupt quickness. With hands on her hips, curiosity abounding, she nevertheless had marvelous legs, inviting hips, and hallmark cheekbones that for a fifty-year-old widow sat up as high and as mighty as hope. The loose wires came onto more serious play. They frisked, they gamboled. Static climbed the air.

Slow Purple pointed at Rags, talking brightly at him, her voice musical. "You being my agent again, Rags? You capture this man at the airport?" She laughed, a kind snicker of a laugh. "You kidnap this one, too?" She nodded a nod of approval. "You saying he's a new customer, a paying customer?" Her voice was as warm as a sun ray across my brow; throaty laughter sincere and not forced. Smiling deeply, she looked at me the way an old friend fields recognition… no hooks, no curves, no reservations, an open book for readers.

For one moment, believing in a kind of play land of the mind, I did not perceive her as real.

Certain aspects fell and rose. Suddenly, as if informed by another being, another mind, a co-host within my body, I saw that her clothes had not fallen upon her, but were being pushed from inside, the mass of her moving inside pressures. The real parts of her made entry under cover, shaping her, designing her in my mind, thrusting parts onto the field of fabric. Oh, I thought, the fabric of her. The fabric of her. I searched my mind for a caliper of sorts. I found none. In a rare moment of secession, Cricket's slightness fell away in a halting bound.

Inside my psyche, someplace elemental, aching against unknown edges, I was conscious again of the existent hole, a black and unnatural hole that had been hanging around for a long time. Yet I had no tool or gauge to measure it, its depth, its width, its emptiness, and that lack of measurement bothered me endlessly. But the hole was there, drawing on me with tenacity. How long I had been aware of its nature, I could no longer remember.

There was conveyance, however. Her house, from that moment, became the bridge from the void within me, my passage outbound. I shook her hand. Felt her eyes. So, in short order, after Slow Purple accepted me as a new boarder and with the same conditions as set up with Rags, the tools came to my hands, the artful tools, the powerful tools, the tools unused by me for so long. And I realized there was something undefined about her, not so mysterious or purely feminine, but an unknown quality that came off all her parts. I might call it an aura, but I might be mistaken, yet it had a glow coming at me with force.

Energy gathered, as from a storm, in one grand hurry. The fence came down, the fence went up. The flagpole came down; the flagpole went up, to stand keen as a white arrow. The old front porch, torn from its moorings against the house, at my hand became a new spread thing, a gateway in itself; new deck and railings, new balusters, steps, white paint where white was wanted, schemed at colors otherwise. And flower boxes, a neat half dozen to each side, bright red ones to boot, bloomed almost instantly against the house. On another morning I stripped away the front

40

door and replaced it, a whole new entryway including all the side lights of Colonial glass framing the doorway.

And every move I made, with every tool employed by an unearthed energy not used in a long time, Slow Purple was at the end of the line as I sized things up; straight lines or curves where curves became important. Whenever I set a line only for my eyes, Slow Purple from the other end smiled back at me her agreement, her warmth in fabric, a part of herself delivered each time. It was the everlasting gender push and I sweated with pleasure. The blue in her eyes sent accord, sent acceptance, sent messages. A hip, one morning at window replacement, cocked me back into the everlasting dreams, her legs, strong and tanned in white shorts, urging movement. The aura at work. Static. The wires connecting again and again. Slow Purple had a way of saying yes without saying yes, a gift if there ever was one. She could freeze me in place when she sat with her solid legs crossed, a hemline stretched. But I was in no hurry. I bent evermore to the task; the tools had recalled me and the job remained.

For sideline work, for diversion, to push my thoughts afield, I taught Rags how to drive again, in a rental pick-up truck, the straight line from the house to the local building supply center, gave directions, took hints, made adjustments, cocked my eye on a new line, saw agreement and accord, felt the light descending or rising some way, somehow. He found old traits and tricks again, and I became new.

A great listener, a student, Rags smiled endlessly, nodded, spoke little, silently gloried as a matchmaker. He was like Barry Fitzgerald, in his black topper, at the same prospects. "Sure, you swing that hammer like a demon, Tools. A regular little demon of energy. Oh, I could rent you out, but that would not be favorable to the lady of the house." He sounded extraordinarily like Barry positioning himself in *The Quiet Man*.

Then, one bright morning, I was rocked! It happened overnight. In one leap it ran through me, knocking things out of place, knocking others where they should have been all along with this job; I was in love again. It came before the sun was up. It came before being fully awake. It impelled me from bed half asleep, urgent, leaning on the day all ready.

41

And I quickly marked the contradictions that flooded the recent empty me: there were things inside loosening up, while others tightened; I knew Slow Purple in my room while she was in the kitchen or at the other side of the house at a task; caught the most basic odors of her from her room or where she passed by in the hallway, and those lifted with flowers coming in from the porch. She was everywhere, and making things happen.

From all the way where love hides and plays its eternal games, it had burst upon me. Breath caught itself in my throat, at first threatening me, and then letting go, knowledge flowing free. And Cricket, lovely thin Cricket, Cricket going to waste, Cricket from too many long nights alone, said it was okay. From all the way out there, where she hung out, she said it was okay. I walked into the kitchen where the sun burst around us, everything in the room lit up; including Slow Purple and me. In the glow of a golden slab of light, eyes searching my eyes for acceptance, all the fabrics of her moving the will of her body, we acknowledged our distinct needs.

The emptiness in me was gone. Cricket had called it away. Willed it away, oh the wiles she had. Cricket, out there wherever, waving goodbye, telling me again and again it was okay, moving my hands the way they moved for her, a touch and a stroke carrying my whole person with it. No man had ever been as lucky as me… and here I was with a second chance. She waved to me, Cricket did, and was gone.

Slow Purple, as beautiful as they come, turned her face to me, eyes wide and alert. Her lips, pink and puffy message centers, parted slowly to let more of the message escape. She took my hand home. Then she came fully into my arms, the warmth from wherever, the powerful frailty that is a woman in love.

We did not talk; we accepted.

A Kommando Loose in Maine

Jaeger Brecht believed he could be anybody, and sound like anybody; he could preach what he practiced. Hot August of 1944 clamped down around him, three or four miles beyond the fence of the POW prison camp near Houlton, Maine. Jaeger Brecht, escapee, was headed for Oxbow, perhaps fifty miles away through the forest and, hopefully, a girl he had not seen since 1932.

He would become again what she had known.

A stiff breeze put a chill on the back of his neck despite the heat. But he was free and in a thick forest, almost like being at home in Bavaria. Semi-darkness brought solitude and time for thinking. Fragrance from balsam fir trees sneaked into his senses and reality and recognition crept into him; his chest nearly burst with expectation coming slowly in waves. For the last five months he'd been nothing but a *kriegsgefangen*, a prisoner of war, with no shackles but confined behind a high wire fence, time sitting its weight on his back, but now he was free... *Obersleutnant* Jaeger Brecht of the *Werwolf*, the *Jagd-Kommando,* with a gifted command of languages, an artful eye for mimicry, and free in the world.

It was about time!

When he questioned how he had managed all this, appraising the last dozen hours among other elements of time, Brecht knew the answer... he was a soldier, right down to bone and the marrow, every last ounce. Luck, he believed, had no part in it at all... not in any of this get-away-quick stuff. And, on the plus side, he was more than a soldier; he was a Kommando. He was special. This POW thing was but a momentary disgrace; he'd see to that. Precision, planning and precision, were cut and dried for a soldier. Cut and dried, he'd make his way home.

And all these years in uniform he had remembered Liza Van Dammen, who once in glory days of 1932 visited relatives in Bavaria. She was the prettiest girl he had ever seen. They had spent the summer together, pushed into each other's lap by their parents. The effects of one war were not over for the mere youngsters while another war loomed across the face of Europe.

This new threat was followed by *All Things German* in general: the Lindberg kidnapping in America, Germany yet smoldering down to its roots from the last war, Hitler and the Nazi party making dire noises in the cellars and byways and back alleys of Berlin, Nazi newspapers inciting riots between Nazis and Communists, Hermann Goering being elected president of the Reichstag, and much of Europe holding its collective breath.

With all that background the young German and the young American escaped into each other. They were young and beautiful. At sixteen, under a moon and beside a lake, they made love, each for the first time. In that initial madness they made love every night for a week pending her return home. Imagination carried them to undreamt horizons, undreamt realities. She had never known such passion; he had never seen such whiteness or imagined such hunger, how it carried from one day to the next. World-wide hysterias in the making welcomed their loving, made a place for it even as history gathered speed by the day. A small island with only two trees on it, in the middle of a lake, served as their trysting place; each day they rowed out and back, to and from love, from and to the world. Later, from home, for months on end, passion close in her fingertips, spelling it out, she wrote religiously, letters full of love and poetry, erstwhile promises and mountains of hope, until he replied that he had joined the army and would have difficulty communicating with a girl in America. In due time it would become *verboten.*

In the army, as his role in it developed, he was too busy to miss her letters. In the states, back in Oxbow, Maine, she was afraid to write; the German touch, and all it promised to carry in the coming years, piled too fully on her.

Part way through his appraisal in the forest, Brecht affirmed his stance, a belief in his rigorous self; he was a soldier, *yea und fur immer*, who happened to need a change of clothes, a proper walking stick, a knife for protection, different shoes, and a girl who could remember passion. Food would come to the hungry in a straightforward manner, a snare, a club, theft in the night. Survival against all odds had been his army course. The targets and obstacles came listed in his mind. But recently, relayed from the guards at the camp, he heard the hard and unbelievable words

44

that German army officers had tried to kill Hitler. How often would chance intervene in his plans, in other's plans? Was it luck that Liza's family had settled in Maine? Was it luck when he said to one snotty American officer, "Please don't send me to Maine. It's too cold there." He could prime the innocents. It was his duty. Acquiescence and good fortune rose from the ploys in his acting.

Again he thought of her at the lake, how he had been suffused with her beauty. For nearly a week the moon had been their bounty, laying its gold on them, touching their blood with a long reach. She had a certain neatness that called on him, but she held to no routine in her lovemaking, nothing neat or coy about her passion. And when he cupped her breasts the first time, he was frozen in place. All the parts stayed with him. It was as though a picture had been taken by his hand, then by his mouth.

Yet he had not taken seriously the poetry that she wrote, and now, bound by forest, he was scrambling to remember some of the lines Liza had written. Not much came back to him, a few straggly lines of little import, a few tender words. Of course, those words now gained new relevance. Perhaps she kept some of that love; he would have to rekindle all of it; it would be required. After his quick review, hungry, miserable in dirty prison clothes, he headed for thicker woods, the pine scent, sent all the way from Bavaria, drawing him on. On the plus side he was able to count on a few tools: Even in his present condition he had impeccable use of English, which, with a little practice, he could use to modulate a northern New England dialect, also impeccable in delivery. For kicks, he could become anybody. Three of the guards at camp had been perfect targets for him, and he aped them to a "T."

Innumerable times he could hear the echo of his nasal and abrupt rendition of "Ayuh," the exact way he had heard other service people, "Maniacs," he was told. who used it continually in his presence. Each time he was imbued with not only a declaration, but a veritable truth: When he was on stage, he was the supreme actor. Comfort normally came to him in solitude, and deep woods meant solitude. It was the best place for thinking; but it was here where the word about army officers planning to assassinate Hitler had freed a small stream of doubt. All of it had to be put together.

Back at the camp, everybody believed he was a plain Wehrmacht soldier, oblivious of the "big picture," a corporal as dumb as they come. That mimicry he could carry off as well as any role. Yet behind him sat a dozen successful trips behind Allied lines, which had been completed before his capture. And currently a map of Maine sat in his head, where he could see lakes and rivers over the long run of the state, and one small town that might house the only chance he had for true escape. It had been a half dozen years since his parents had received letters from Liza's parents because of the war, but he remembered looking at a map of the state back then, the romance of far places playing tunes with his imagination.

Brecht kept recounting himself, reforming old strengths after imprisonment, after escape. There was a time he dotted every *I* and crossed every *T* that came his way. His uniform, crisp and clean at any hour, could be hung and worn again an hour later, fresh as a newborn. The medals on his chest were lustrous, and warranted; in the eyes of many he'd been a hero, courageous, a courtier of death in any sense, and palatable to the broad spectrum of the Nazi media at home.

Far at home.

He was a product of his times, and now he breathed the air and the scent of the forest, the rush of fragrant balsam fir trees and white spruce, now and then some sugar maple. In a new valley a new smell rose on the wind, perhaps honey bees working their tails off. Hunger, though it would tend to govern his actions, would have to stand in line, wait its turn. He'd live off the land, but shun roads, railroads, the curves and shores of lakes and rivers, even minor streams where anglers might play their secret pools. The balsam fir trees that surrounded him were much like the Norway spruce and silver fir of the Bavarian forests. Here as there, animals would feed off the trees, the moose, the squirrels, the white-tailed deer. He had all ready seen crossbills and chickadees. Sufficient food would be found in his line of march.

Behind him, though, the war was a shambles, had become too messy even in the planning. He had seen it coming, the way little sins were allowed to become cardinal errors in life, positions, even in armor and supplies, all across the face of Europe and in all the battle zones. He'd been behind the lines in North Africa, and Italy, and captured in France; the world was shrinking for Germany, a chokehold growing with daily reports circulating in the camp; the Allies in Paris, American paratroopers in his favored St. Tropez, the vast machine of the German army now susceptible.

The escape from the camp had been a solo effort from the outset. As usual, he had difficulty in finding comrades worthy of chance and charade; they had become too comfortable, too chatty and ingratiating with their wardens. The Americans at the camp were too generous, almost forgiving in their daily work, turning their backs on minor transgressions, letting footholds develop. All this was crucial to him as he planned his escape; he had to trust the Americans' easy manners, their obscene laziness. Only the sergeant with the hard eyes and the dark birth mark on half his face would be a worthy opponent.

He could remember his first mission, leaving timed explosives in a fuel dump after he had walked right past a dolt of a guard, saying the C.O. had sent him for a battery replacement for his Jeep. "Shit, man, they send me back from my recon outfit because I fucked up and I end up a fucking nursemaid for some asshole 90-fucking-day wonder. Will wonders never cease?" He had slipped his arm over the guard's shoulder and then slipped the knife in the guard's gut, twisting it home. War is hell, he had thought as the knife made its way through flesh, encountered bone, turned again in his hand. War is hell. He almost said, "Son," seeing the young face of the guard as it passed by him heading into eternity. Valhalla, he might have whispered, hearing old brass echoes, Wagner beating about in his own blood. Excitement in the handle of the knife. He'd have to watch the ounce of sentiment that played at his backside, like a dash of condiment long forgotten on the shelf, but holding its true flavor.

Nights were as bad as war, as all the gathered acts mounted for his review. Often he prayed for forgiveness, but he had been commissioned for this, this way of making his way in the world, and the war… he was a sneak, a thief, an impersonator, but an actor who one day would be on the world's finest stages, his name on marquees, in headlines, women aching for his torso. He saw himself in London, Moscow, Paris, New York, stepping out in

47

front of the lights, Hamlet, Lear, old Hal himself, and he would bring all his past with him... every damned ounce of it. Berlin would be his own, a thespian's town, his town. Yet he was aware the war would never leave him, the scars as deep as blood and then deeper, his knife as keen as the one in a surgeon's hand, just as sharp and just as deadly.

Immersed in thought, caught up in himself by an impulsive idea, and emerging from a thick patch of brush, he was halted by the sight of an old man slowly plodding on a slightly worn trail twenty or so yards across an open glade. A fishing rod pointed upward over one shoulder and a creel hung on the opposite hip. Across his chest, a bandolier of lures, sat the ammunition of a fly fisherman. Brecht felt a pinch of recognition; the man looked like his grandfather, who might have worn the same gear and the same clothing as he set out for a day of fishing; the lumberjack shirt buttoned to the collar, sleeves cuffed and buttoned, corduroy pants making a music he could almost hear.

How far had the man come on this path? Was there a fishing cabin nearby? Did he have companions? Reluctance overcame Brecht as he withdrew from possible sight; the slight recognition of pleasure was erased. All his training took over; if he made a mistake, relaxed a moment too long, he would end up paying for it. He could not suffer himself to be so indulgent; it would mark him a loser. *There shall be no confrontations,* were words and beliefs he must stand by; he could not be enticed, pleased, excited by any ordinary contact... ordinary contacts can carry such inordinate revelations. Be ever alert, he affirmed again and again. Ever alert. You are a soldier. A Kommando!

Thoughts of Liza could not be allowed to imperil him, he avowed. Yet the thoughts of her had crossed his mind, at the ends of flighty reveries... on the island, between the two pine trees, her all around him, and their passion buried in the moon's yellow prison. Her richness came back at a moment's notice. Those were moments he fell into a beautiful Hell.

Ah, Kommando, he said, Life moves on, and the island disappeared and the twin trees and the yellow moon, and the throb deep inside, the sense of pushing on a body, and the body pushing back.

Some hours later, in a small dale full of shade and sweet smells, he saw a flicker of life, and a doe rose slowly, looking about as if for directions or odor detection. For a short time he felt her sheer and innocent beauty. It was knocked aside by the thought of someone, like himself, feasting on her meat. "Life is made that way, Cookie," he softly muttered, in practice of his on-stage presence.

One movement of his hand to his mouth, him at full surprise, and the doe bolted off, a white flash leaving her signature. Bird calls came from the orchestra of shade above him, probably set off by the doe, everything in the forest caught up in linkage of one sort or another, life spelling itself out. He thought he'd best be aware of the connections, for he was now in the chain of life that the forest sustained. Animals, like the deer and moose, and every sort of bird, must live on and off the trees and brush and herbs that spread their arms in a thousand ways. Back at the camp, whenever talk about the forest opened up by guards or support personnel, he absorbed all he could, filing it away for later use. Now he was at that "later," and it was not luck that brought him this far, not in any manner.

Often he wondered how he'd find Liza, or how he'd *find* her... what memories for her were still vivid, recollective, favored? Too much had passed between them, even in spite of the years without word. Images came at him, forced up from below by her personal richness, which, he had to admit, had never been experienced again. But she was merely an out now, a means to an end, and the weight of that sudden judgment beat its way into his mind. He absorbed his own punishment, yet realized it was a bare rationalization; he could be good at that.

On the other hand, animal life abounded, as part of the forest choir; birds at all levels of the scale were resonant in the thick trees all around, as if he were in a large aviary in Berlin or some other cosmopolitan center. Nature's introduction was progressing with a full texture of song and secret sounds coming from deeper, darker or higher places in copse and thicker growths.

A small stream at one place came into a small glade and he pictured a pond or a lake behind it, pushing at the mouth of this stream. Hunger was stirring in his gut and the black flies were extremely aggravating. Security shot uppermost in his mind, though; keeping out of sight, gambling for food only when absolutely necessary, creature comforts, all in abeyance, being the least of his yearnings. Two hours later he had found a change of clothes in a small cabin at the edge of a pond sitting in a small valley with an L shape. One end of the pond, he was sure, could not be seen from the other end. He found pants with a blue stripe, a blue shirt with a torn pocket, and the treasure of a pair of boots that fit him, though with many miles underfoot. The rutted path to the cabin had been overgrown to a point it looked unused for many months. He had sat quietly behind a row of trees watching it for hours. The wait produced in the cabin, besides the clothes, a can of salt sitting on a shelf, whose contents he wrapped in foil; a bottle of catsup that he left for the next tenant or visitor; and a can of tuna fish. The tuna fish, saturated in oil, was a treat for him. With care he buried the prison garb under a rock a hundred yards away, the empty tuna can was crushed and thrown into a deep pool of the stream.

A day later, a night's sleep under boughs under his belt, the outlook on escape looked brighter. There was no way she could forget how they had simmered that first night and then burst into week-long flames. And now, he was sure, he was within Oxbow territory. It would not be long.

A week after his escape from the POW camp, Brecht was hiding in the brush behind her house. Everything in sight caught his scrutiny, his measurement. He could have frolicked he felt so good, the fifty or so miles from Houlton were behind him and Maine morning sunlight, the raw power of it, bathed all the structures at this end of a dirt road. In all he counted in proximity of the house a dozen birdhouses hanging from tree branches or sitting atop poles. Three very busy birdhouses sat but a hand's throw from one window of the house and early feeders, a kind he did not know, bounced about like marbles loose in a jar. Each of the three birdhouses appeared newly painted, some even artistically decorated. Only the entrances of each house were dark, and he saw such entrances near eaves of the main house and at the eaves of a large barn. Liza, for sure, was artistic, and that too made him feel good. The Maine sun added to her color schemes as the birdhouses showed off a sense of brilliance, the way art exhibits are seen by a first-time observer.

From where he stood, sundry paths, other than the one he had used, went off in different directions, their trail marks faintly distinct in grass and low brush. Apple trees, among other trees, were scattered around the house as if the house a hundred years earlier had been built in the middle of an orchard. A new aroma, thin as a sheet of air, made him hungry, though he could not identify the odor source. It was as though its identity was creeping up on him and he looked behind him to make sure nothing was nearing his hiding place.

Nothing moved but leaves and birds and the vapor-like waves of unseen heat. Leafy grape vines clung to a series of thin trees and poles and would provide cover when he approached the house. Other structures sat fully in sunlight, lit up from antiquity, all well-worn, having been long put to regular use. There was a barn with repaired doors but a dipping ridge pole, a henhouse of sorts with wire windows, an outhouse between the barn and the house leaning with an odd tilt, a tire hanging from a tree on a length of rope that a bare wind touched slightly, and, finally, an old car rusting at the far end of a small garden plot, young trees at the onset of embracing it. Before long the vehicle, by slow corrosion and tenacious tentacles, would be absorbed into the landscape. He imagined again an old voice, coming from a long distance in the past, saying, "This too shall be dust."

The rustic America Liza had extolled in her visit to Bavaria was there in front of him. Earlier, in false dawn, in an upstairs window in the shadowy morning, he had seen her, had seen her for the first time in a dozen years. Her laughter came back in a heady maneuver, and the sense of vibrancy she had unleashed those dozen years past also returned as he saw her nude with a soft light behind her. Parts of the recall had lain hidden for those years, as if their appearance would knock him out of timing or routine. He was a soldier first, trying for a full escape. Yet, in the morning light, there was an eruption at the sight of her bathed in the yellow sunlight.

If he was able to see her alone, what would he say to her? How would he start? Had it been too long for anything to come out of this trip, all this planning? He shut off that thought and put it away. It would happen. It had to happen.

From behind him, as if from nowhere, motion and near-muted sound, a breath beyond a whisper, arrived at the same time. Brecht, in control, turned slowly, afraid to show surprise, afraid to look suspicious, and saw an old man standing practically in his back pocket. He had heard no approach, not a snapped twig, not a rustled leaf. This old man, a native for sure, and at least 80 for sure, wearing glasses, rubber boots as black as bad mushrooms, carrying a bamboo fishing rod in one hand and a metal tackle box in the other hand, was staring at him. Brown-rimmed spectacles were lopsided on his head, sitting over one ear as if pinched in a way, set awry by a frown. A wide, punished nose, extra broad at the bridge, logged with experience at some kind of physical action, crinkled in curiosity. His eyes were almost hidden in wild eyebrows, thick, black, untrimmed, as dark as they must have been half a century earlier. A wicker creel rode on one hip, part of his uniform. A red and black checkered lumberjack shirt, buttoned closely at each wrist and at his throat, marked neatness and long habit. A large Adam's apple sat atop the neckline button as prominent as a pork loin hanging in a butcher's window.

If the old man were to fall down, Brecht would not be surprised, but he was a survivor and a history of tenacity showed like a written biography; hard chin and jaw line, three dark marks of age on his forehead bigger than usual freckles, the nose a relic from more than one argument, an old daring hanging about in his face, a daring not all used up by any means, and curiosity by the pound.

"You lost, son?" The old man's voice was soft and sure, as though he held the answer to his own question. He could have been a teacher at the head of a classroom, knowing everything behind the lesson. "You knowed someone hereabouts? You knowed Liza?" He marked the clothes that Brecht wore, the boots, the belt buckle, then rested on Brecht's eyes. "You got yourself a name, being for a stranger?"

"Rawlins they call me, whenever it's not late for supper, and then it makes no difference what I'm called." A smile came with his humor, easy as aces as part of his new face. "Yes, I know

52

someone here." He felt he had become a Maine person, and the language and inflections of service personnel back at the camp hung out in whispers for him to cling to. "Never too late for feedin', you might say if you was asked." A minor snort of disdain was added, like needed punctuation.

The man repeated his question, with a hint of surprise caught up in his words. "You knowed Liza?" The old man looked back at the house and the window with a light in it, a window on the second floor, obviously a bedroom window. A shadow moved through glowing light morning was catching up with.

There was an art form to the old man's questioning, as with a teacher at the chalkboard where a poser was marked and the solution salted away for this extreme moment where doubt, question and curiosity were playing games with one another.

Brecht, aware he was the subject of deep appraisal, conjured up an instant liking for the old man, protective of a younger neighbor, unafraid of a younger stranger. He also assumed the old man was a damn good fisherman. The bamboo fly rod was likely as near old as its carrier. Other attributes, maintenance, neatness, proper care of property of any value, came in short order, even as Brecht felt the deep penetration of doubt and curiosity settle into his body.

Carlton Ebbers stood Brecht right up, stiff as a ramrod, when he yelled, "Liza, Carlton Ebbers sittin' out here with this here gent says he knows of you." In the bright morning air, his voice carried clearly to the house.

Her head came fully out the window. "Who is it, Carlton? What's his name?"

"Says his name is Rawlins."

Brecht jumped in, yelling "Jaeger" as clearly as he could. He looked at the old man and said, "Jaeger Rawlins," as if explaining himself.

Liza's voice rang out. "Jaeger! Jaeger! I'll be right out. Give me a minute. It's okay, Carlton. I know him! I know him!"

Liza, in a housecoat, bolted from the back door seconds later, and his name came rushing from her mouth, her lungs, her whole body mass carried in her cries. "Jaeger! Jaeger!" Those cries even shook up old Carlton Ebbers. Across the yard she

53

rushed, birds by the dozens flitting and leaping about from the birdhouses, all in her wake. One hand held the blue robe at her waist. When she stumbled and loosed that hand, both men could see she wore nothing underneath the robe. Carlton Ebbers smiled at old mystery and Jaeger Brecht went all the way back to 1932.

Liza was swept up in Jaeger Brecht's arms, and her arms wrapped around her old lover.

Carlton Ebbers dropped his eyes and then looked off at a piece of the sunrise sitting in the break of balsam firs crowding a small rise. The bamboo fly rod came elevated, then pointed tip first down a path, and he moved off, saying, "I'll leave you folks to rememberin', while I go to fishin'." He was out of sight in a whisper of seconds. Not a note of his departure was heard, as muffled as his approach had been.

They were alone for the first time in twelve years.

Liza strained against Jaeger Brecht, bending against him her whole length, her breath searching for proper space, movement, expression. She inhaled him. Old scents rushed back, imagination running well ahead of them, catching up many of her parts, old touches breathing new life on their own. Came in a maddening rush the magic he once controlled in his hands. "Jaeger. Jaeger, how did you get here?"

"Is anybody in the house?" he said. When he was suddenly hit with her perception of him, he thought caution must be simmered, tempered. "It's so good to see you again, Liza. You're still beautiful, like a flower that's still blooming. May I come in? I need food, I'm famished." Release and rush hit him at the same time. "I'll tell you everything, Liza, but I must rest too. I have been running away for a long time now. I want my running away to be over and done with." Once again he was on-stage. It sounded exactly like the excuse she had wanted, the one that would carry her through dreams, promises, and all accountabilities from the past.

But right then, twisted in the middle of doubt and discovery, Jaeger Brecht didn't know who he was, didn't know who he wanted to be, or was trying to be. She was lovely yet, the remarkable face hardly aged a moment from what it had been. And she was directly from morning freshness, a liberating and

54

innocent freshness. She smelled so good and clean, so unlike his own person, so unlike all those confined in the prison camp. This was a dreamt freedom circulating all around him, this freshness, this newness. He had no idea how long it would last.

"Jaeger, where have you been? What happened to you? You know I've been crazy for you ever since I met you. And all this time, it's been agony, years of agony. What has the war done to you? I prayed for you every day. Every day of my life since then." Her arms had only felt this comfort in that long ago. "Oh, this stupid war." Total moments from the island had come back to her, though she knew they had never been far away. Want, at last, was flooding her, all that pent up want she had controlled for a dozen years.

His beard was rough on her face, the harsh reality of return softening its impact. The one fist of two hands was solid on her back, like determination, like an anvil, hard like a new promise being made. He was older, of course, she thought, but more handsome. A man now, a full grown handsome man, though tired looking, who had come back after all the loneliness. She breathed him in again, a long and deep breath that plummeted down through her body, finding all the old places, the hidden places. A strong scent of her own forestland also rode on his person; there came the balsam and pine and deep wood solace that rode in such aromas, herself a woods person, who would have loved at another time to have gone off with Carlton Ebbers looking for breakfast brookies.

Brecht, as though reading her mind, looked back to where Carlton Ebbers had disappeared into the woodlands, all the alarm systems within him clicking back on. But not a leaf moved, not a pine needle, not a discarded shadow to show that an old man with spectacles askew, and a bamboo fly pole pointing his way through underbrush, had left the scene.

Liza said, "Oh, Carlton's just going fishing on the stream, looking for brookies, looking for breakfast. He'll be gone a few hours, and he usually minds his own business. He was worried about me seeing a stranger here, that's why he yelled out to me. He's a dear neighbor who lives about a mile away. He's always looked out for me ever since." She did not finish that thought.

55

She came alert about her robe and closed it, other instincts crowding her mind and body. She took his hand. "Come in," she said, "please come in. Let me cook for you. You can shower and shave, get a change of clothes. Tell me everything later, the war and all. I hate it. I have hated it since the day it started." Her hands pulled at him. "Nobody else is home. My parents died within months of each other from the same accident. Five years ago. My aunt and uncle live here with me, in my house, but they've gone to visit a son in Vermont and a grandson who is going off to the army next month. He's just turned 18. He's a boy, a mere boy."

He showered, shaved, dressed in comfortable clothes she had found in a quick search. Sunlight poured into the room through two windows facing east, the rays falling across a table with a red and white checkered tablecloth, and spilling onto the floor. She had kicked her slippers loose and they sat in the sunlight, being measured, optioned. He thought about her legs and what he remembered of their shapely presence. Now they lined up faintly behind the fabric of her robe. She cooked at a huge black stove that filled a corner of the room, her feet bare, telegraphic. A vase of flowers stood in the middle of the table. Other vases and potted plants crowded the two windowsills. Their aromas fought their way through bacon odor. When he sat to eat he kept looking at her still in her robe, the bacon rolled into itself, the eggs like sunrise on the plate, coffee kicking him in the gut. But her freshness kept coming back to him. As she stepped near him, he put his arms around her, felt her quickness, felt her shaking as if she had never stopped shaking from the island. He did not eat. They went off to her bed. They loved the morning away. He told her everything. "I've been a soldier. If I've been nothing else in all this time, I was a soldier. I had a duty. I did my duty. I was good at it. I was very good at it until I was taken prisoner."

Liza, reveling in Brecht's arms, still inhaling the now and the past in splendid return, said, "Do you know German army officers tried to kill Hitler, tried to bomb him?" She added, "With complete justification," as if she was accenting both their stands on the issue. "Do you know what an evil he has become?" There was no way around it, the war had to be mentioned repeatedly, with Hitler right in the mix of it, even as she enjoyed the slightest touch of Brecht's hands, the smell of him, the corners of his mouth the way he said some words, as if he was trying to relax back into something old, something believable, a lifetime recaptured.

"That has bothered me lately, and a great deal. I don't know who has betrayed me, my officers, my leaders in the army, or Hitler himself. All these days in the forest by myself, running, hiding from fishermen, stealing property, it has preyed on me. Now I find you again. When they brought me to the camp at Houlton, the day I arrived, I've thought of nothing but you since then. Thought of nothing but getting here. To see you. To be free."

"Oh, Jaeger, you can stay here with me until the war is over. You can be my cousin Rolf from Sweden, a true neutral. We can say you lost your papers, or something. We can fool all of them. My aunt and uncle know all about you. I told them almost everything. They know how much I've missed you. You can learn how to farm, tend chickens and pigs, be free, go fishing with me." She laughed, the joy flooding hers senses. "We can go fishing for breakfast brookies, do them up in corn meal, drop an egg in place, pumpernickel toast, smell morning coffee in the woods like we're being mesmerized." Her smile flashed her exposed soul. She had almost said, "Like we're married."

All her lost years ran into each other, at the exact same time as Carlton Ebbers was talking to the sheriff in Oxbow. His face was red, he was out of breath and his fishing gear dropped someplace back in the Oxbow forest, thrown aside as he marched his way to the center of town.

"You better shake a leg on this, Harold. Don't go dallyin' on me. I tell you now, will tell them in court if that's what you're worried about, that this man is probably the escaped German POW from Houlton we been hearin' about on the radio. He has this here hair cut too short for the likes of Oxbow. There's a line right across the tops of his ears, like a Marine haircut, like a German Army haircut. Liza probably knows him from someplace, like from a visit back there years ago. Her father used to talk about it at the inn. She has a heart for him, that I'm damn sure of. Near collapsed in his arms. Don't near do that with strangers, not none of our girls."

"What the hell do you know about a German army haircut, Carlton, and young love for that matter? You were even too old back there all the way to 1917. Too old now. My god, man, we got to have more than a guess on this. The Flatlanders would laugh us silly if we get smoke out of no fire on such stuff. Besides all the to-do we'd shake out of the trees, I hear we'll have more than a million people in the state tonight watchin' the solar eclipse old Mother Nature has planned for us. Be awful crowded for laughs."

The whole deck of cards was snug up Carlton Ebbers' sleeve. "Well, Harold, I'll just have to tell you what kicked it all the way in for me. Comin' here I went to my Walter's fishin' cabin on the Nighthawk, near The Toe Line Lodge, and those there duds that Liza's friend is wearin' belong to my son. I gave them to him for extra fishin' clothes for his cabin, dryin' out stuff. My old police pants, my old shirt, even my old boots. I'd know them anyplace, with the patch Elbert Derrin stitched in where the 'coons wanted to eat the fatty sweat outta one a them one night. Them boots're not where they're supposed to be. He's not about to march them right on past me, girl or no girl. No sir, not at all, not with my grandson Alfred over there right on the edge of Germany this here damned minute."

The sheriff of Oxbow nodded his agreement to the old man.

Miss Magnusson and the Druggist

So it was, when I sauntered away from visiting dear comrades at the veterans section of our Riverside Cemetery, my mind and my mind's eye searching for faces *sainting* me for another day, I saw Mabel Magnuson's name on an edge-withered gray tombstone a dozen yards off the road. I remembered the lady in a flash of light. When whatever instant agony came upon her, she'd have eyes darker than an owl; my dark-haired seventh grade teacher burdened, it seemed to me from first call, born to carry armfuls of pain in her eyes.

Hurry, Thomas! she'd say. *The druggist.*

That deep registry of torment had done it. Again!

As happens when you get knocked out of the ordinary, the riches of your past come flooding home with the slightest effort. Now and then there is no need for exertion; shapes, silhouettes, shadows coming off as close to substance as you can imagine.

Her stone slab was deeply faded and worn in comparison to those impersonal blocks in company with it; the nearby monuments sharper, clearer, granite standing finally at ease the way a cutter first leaves it with high intent. Every edge of her tombstone, as a result, came rough and abrasive on my eye. I suspect that *that* abrasiveness was for attention, the way her name loafed and rounded into shape, almost touched back at me harmlessly and with a soft echo and a small call from way off in memory. *Mabel Magnuson,* the antiqued headstone said, my eye or attentive and sympathetic ear catching the alliteration first, the half phonetics secondly.

Such granite markers talk, have special messages of their own. You may not warrant an attitude exists about tombstones, or their messages, unless you take me for my bounden word, even as I vouch now that I was walking among spirits, some of them by acquaintance, some of them not. Mabel Magnuson, early in my life, had been pivotal to me and, as it would prove at once, hand-out helpless.

I heard the echo: *Hurry, Thomas! The druggist.*

Her tombstone was at an angle to my line of sight, yet carried a vector with it, where some elder plotter of this huge span of gravesites managed to squeeze it between a maple tree almost a yard across in the bole and a large mausoleum of colder, older granite. Punched for eternity into the mausoleum's mounded and entirely obtuse face rested a heavy metal door frozen as much by idleness as by rust. Out loud it said this rugged monument was a place where one might register immediately and with sadness the end of a family's reign, perhaps the last scion long past put to bed for the final nap. Loneliness, it was. Finality. I was thinking of last things first and first things last scanning the area of Miss Magnuson's resting place, only the silence broken.

Hurry, Thomas! The druggist.

Perhaps it's like the single pin in an alley when the bowler takes dead aim and makes a head-on hit; the pin flying close to smithereens, the ball plowing through like an old race car. That's how I felt even on a day full of new blooms and old friends; green, warm, wondrous it was, and me knocked asunder by her latest summons.

Saugus had spread itself apart in this morning's mad scurry, noisy from a distance, busy at sound and motion of people in the mix of the day, my swearing I could hear the truck tires racing on the turnpike nearly a mile away. Recess's high chattering from my old school a few hundred yards away came as joyful and as mournful as old train whistles across a wide valley hankering to be heard, like the Route of the Phoebe Snow or the old Rock Island Line coming back. Fully alert I was, open, as avaricious as ever for fact or folly or whatever this day had dreamed up.

As part of my daily constitutional, my healthy walk about town, I had called on a few comrades at rest for as much as a half century, and more in some cases, to say a few words of continuity. The promise had been made, by me, that I would not forget them, not in my *ever*. That promise, here recorded, had been the dedication of a book of mine: "For those who have passed through Saugus, those comrades who bravely walked away from home and fell elsewhere, and the frailest imaginable soldier of all, frightened and glassy-eyed and knowing he is hapless, one foot onto the soil at D-Day or a statistical sandy beach of the South Pacific and going down, but not to be forgotten, not here."

However long that *ever* or *never* would prove to be was up to these constitutionals, the doctors as would eventually come upon me, and life and its clash of vagaries. I was, for my comrades, firm with promise.

The maples are broad and sweeping now, I'd tell my them in short conversations at each site, saying their names over and over, finding a facial characteristic to grasp, eyes paired beneath a half brow, a nose abridged, a clipped earlobe, the way a lip dragged its mouth down at one corner sharp as a curse, like as on Mouse Marshall's mouth in the pool hall at an opponent's good shot. Now and then, on a slight sheet of air, usually cool and welcome, there'd be a word or two, an oath, a solid hurrah for grand surprise or occasion. *Attention*, it would be said, and thus said and done.

So often in return leaped a small incident being carried by a corner or an edge of the incident, as I read the dates on their flat memorials stained by tossed grass, wet leaves, or bird droppings, all part of time's dread camouflage. Life's plane geometry let them flood back into my consciousness suddenly absorbing last moments more than fifty years long in the teeth. In support of their presence, their own make-up and attention to detail, I'd carry on about aromas and new scents bristling along the edge of the cemetery, what birds I recognized by color or voice, the whispers urged by gasoline engines coming off the main road, telling each one that I am still able to identify a Ford or a Chevie by motor tendencies, and proving it. Hey, guys, I'd offer, it'll be warm for a while. It'll be months before the leaves redden for the winter toss, and then go flamboyant and pyrotechnic.

Also, by invention, I'd let them know occasionally and sadly that I'd found, much later in my life, some of them had rushed by to get out of my way, while others hardly as interesting are yet rumbling and sauntering happily on their way wherever. None of these noble correspondents were ever particularly put out by my offerings. None of them ever questioned the amplitude of my descriptions. No one found me wanting at the wrong season. I'd tell them the children at recess, where we first met in many instances, were from this shared perspective still riotously gay and free, shrill voices coming on the breath of wind, like an invasion at the beachhead mimicking movement.

Parkie, the Sahara Kid, rested here. And both Wingsy and the mad red-headed boxer Eddie Mac, the Korean Kids, who died a year apart in Korea and lie now but a grave apart, every so often calling me out in the night. More than a dozen teammates also occupied the holy ground, the same strata inhabited for sixty years by my seventh grade teacher, Mabel Magnuson.

Her worn gravestone said things too.

Hurry, Thomas! The druggist.

Recollection is an imp, a devilish counterpart of the mind, an upstart, yet a seer of what makes me *me*.

The first call of Mabel Magnuson came back to me harsh as a gunshot as I ambled down the curving road of the cemetery, noting other names on other headstones, forgetting them in an instant, scratching for knowledge, known names, in most cases bringing with them nothing at all. That's a reverse sadness, not finding the names of friends petrified on stone. Perhaps it's perverse, when you really think about it. I didn't wish anything on anybody, just for recognition; but most names were alien to me.

But back at school, then, it was another May day, the outside looming brightly at window and doorway entry; maple odors leaping the way birds leap from limb to limb, flowers at riot, the myth of baseball with a music all its own, sending its relentless cries and echoes. I sat in the rear of Miss Magnuson's classroom, second row from the back, behind dark-haired Bimper Mahany with her freckles imported or emigrated from Ireland, beside humorless Buddy Trottingham from Nottingham and robust Arthur Lauria on loan, apparently, from an Italian barbershop. In a few short months, it seemed, the barber's son would sport dark hair on his chin, the first of our class. Behind me sat Charlie Flann, a survivor of infantile paralysis, a swift but knock-kneed runner who even then could pick them up and put them down with astonishing alacrity, to whom I would say goodbye to sixty years hence on my front steps one day as he sought out old time's sake.

At geography we were, or at least the spread map of the world now finds a spot in my mind, and the maples, so close, were broadcasting their scent and that of the coming summer. I heard

Miss Magnuson say, to this day I swear in a whispered but insistent manner, "Thomas! Thomas!"

Twice, on this spring day full of hope and escape, I was summoned. Out of a soft therapy of sounds and smells I was summoned. 'Thomas," I heard. I heard it again. "Thomas."

It was not Bimper, for she'd called me Tommyrot from day one, nor Buddy Trottingham, nor pal Charlie at my backside. When I looked up front, Miss Magnuson was crooking a finger at me. Blackness filled her eyes, a whole field of it in stark recall, and solidified her face, emanated from her whole person. But, like a free clue to a mystery, she nodded a look as if to say, "You read that right. Come up here now. I do have need, Thomas." Then I saw her lips say, "Please hurry."

With a sense of acute awareness demanding support, I searched Miss Magnuson's eyes and found what accompanied her voice. Disappointment I'd read in another's eyes before that moment, the way my mother could broadcast it, stated but unsaid. I could never recall seeing pain in a person's eyes before that moment, no matter in what guise or give because people hold back too often the things they want to say about pain, unless it was a sissy. But I saw it then. I did not attend at the moment of that communiqué the dark blue dress she wore every Tuesday, or the set of pearls usually about her neck with that repeated dress, pearls she often said in geography lessons had been lifted as treasure from a Pacific atoll. What I saw were her eyes, rimmed and owl dark, like old pie plates.

Miss Magnuson was hurting and the pain almost screamed in those dark sanctuaries. I knew I was being measured and I swear I could have melted, but when I neared her desk she placed her hand on mine. "Please hurry, Thomas," she said. "Go down to Mr. Brecht's drug store. Give him this note. Run as fast as you've ever run in your life. Please, Thomas, run, run! Don't look back. Bring back what he gives you." Then she used a big word that came all the way home for me. "I implore you," she said, her mouth moving, her lips moving, as if annunciating for a deaf person and the plea leaped right out of her face. She folded the note into my hand and said again, her voice too in dark sorrow and quick emergency, "Hurry, Thomas! Hurry!"

63

Those words haunted me for the next two months, the balance of the school year. In my sleep I would hear the sound of them, see the depth in her face, her mute lips drawing the words for sensations, feel the clutch penetrating my soul, grasping. Why did she pick me, I wondered, where some of the others flew like the wind on the field, where they'd call me Snowshoes, slower than Tillie's molasses in an ice storm. I never told anybody about my missions, secretive, in trust, trusted out of all my classmates, always wondering why me.

Of course, lack or speed or not, I never knew the cargo I carried back from Mr. Brecht's store on the corner of Jasper Street two blocks from the school, now and then in a slim tube or a sealed envelope, probably whatever was at hand for the quick delivery. Never once did Mr. Brecht question me, cast an alert or an aspersion, never suppressed an oath, surely never tendered any advice or warning in tone or manner. Never was I refused the simple service, the understanding nod, and the acceptance of small terror or pain, the whole world beyond his means at some kind of suffering. More than a few times he'd leave a customer in the midst of business to take care of me and my mission, a questioning hand in the air, a shrug of complacency from some people. Whenever I entered his store it was an alarm sounding, for I made that run for Miss Mabel Magnuson at least ten times that seventh year of my education, and the first year of mortal knowledge.

Hurry, Thomas! Hurry!

It occurred to me as I wound down the curving road of the cemetery, away from last call with comrades and old pals, that the solution never surfaced with me, never came up for air. I never knew what caused her pain, her panic, her urgency. I suppose now in experienced attention it might have been a newly-found disease that had dropped its foul hand on her. Maybe migraine's deep thunder bolt-thick and wide as the sky I have since seen clapping a friend or two exactly behind the eyeballs, or some other mad tool of mortality inserted into the soul of that woman.

Charlie Brecht's hair, to freshen memory, was black as a lagoon, while his complexion sat pink as a new rose on the vine. Dark glass frames made caricature of his face, disarming customers at the outset, putting common fears to rest. Among the

64

souls of his trade he rose as an honest and totally warm soul. So many times, for innumerable causes in favor of youngsters and active teen agers, he had gone out of his way. Those efforts cost him money and a bit of reputation with a few odd sorts who specialized in rumor, but when he passed on I know he must have been a happy man, sad only for what he had not accomplished in his life.

When that first note of many was delivered by my hand, Charlie looked down at the scripture, looked back into my being, measured, accepted, and scurried behind the wall separating ice cream sodas and sundaes and odd cone colors from bottles and vials and pills of every order and disorder. It was a mahogany wall, or a dark wall at best, the part facing me and all customers being the back of a series and levels of small drawers built into the other side, tiers of them.

Mysteries abided there behind that wall, I had heard, cures and blessings sent upon the ailing, the elderly, and the unknown, those who hailed from all the corners of the town. For some, it was sure, Charlie was saint and savior, often hand-delivering a potion or a solution to pain or just plain-out misery when he closed his store down for the night. Until this day, whenever his name is mentioned, the elders among us nod with appreciation of the druggist with the pink complexion and the dark glasses, and bound to be blessed.

Yet, here I lingered in self-shot photos almost fifty years later worried about the fate of a teacher long absent. In the shift of mixing ideas swiftly came back the search for an old schoolmate, Hugh Menzies, now parallel with comrade Eddie McCarthy and those two graves separated by a stranger, one grave apart. He had been gone for a similar extravagance of age and my lifetime, and had been found, or the then current news of his demise came revealed only with the assistance of an advertisement in a military organization magazine.

With a monstrous nerve alive inside me, shorting on my soul, I wondered in what direction, what new vector, I could turn to for discovery of Mabel Magnuson's departure. The face of pain kept coming back, as if demanding it be closed down in my mind. For weeks her visage haunted me, then went on into months, and brought me to her stone each time my comrades invited me back for a visit, their being relentless through spring burst, summer torpor, autumn ignition, winter stillness. There was no way for me to know that she was hearing any of my graveside chatter, never mind accepting it. No reply in any order, no look askance, no dimming to lighter gray of her owl-dark eyes.

Naught but silence came, accompanied by the frozen mobility of Mabel Magnuson. Oh, nothing the way my pals let me know they were listening. No answer of a sly look from Parkie once after scoring with a town beauty, his face as alive as it would ever be, the cleft on his chin almost chattering a sense of accomplishment, his eyes locked on mine the same night at the Meadowglen Club when he said, looking over the top of a bottle of beer, "Man, you're fucking literate"; or the usually stoic Victor D.'s uncontrollable grin at a great hand in poker; or, lastly on a high and sad note, hearing Eddie M. repeat a tenor's brilliance at *Danny Boy* at a party, blonde Gracie at his side all the minutes of his life.

Nothing of the sort.

I went looking.

Old obits revealed little more than the dates cut on her stone. No children succeeded her in a house half a dozen times remade and sold. Confreres too had idled away leaving few tracks, if any, back to that school on the side of the hill and a stone's throw from the cemetery, and to names of teachers gone into thinnest air. Only a chance remark to a friend… who happened to drop the remark in front of an elderly aunt who knew a lady who knew a lady… found history.

The last lady in the line of knowledge was just short of being delivered to a nursing home by a niece whose hands were now tied and spirits sagging with too many tasks. Three times now she had to call on neighbors to get the lady back into her bed, and once had to call help from the fire department. I could feel her plight, and my thirst ran it a good race.

Ethel Packard brightened at my face even before I dropped a few questions in her lap.

I had been told that her body was failing miserably, but that she was as sharp as she had ever been, and "with wit and charm," I had also been advised. "Ethel Packard may be one of the nicest ladies you will ever meet, her own lady and has always been so." A slightest lift of one eyebrow carried its own weight of announcement. Some thoughts, supposedly between the lines, create the soundest curiosity, offer a slash of objectivity. My interest was revved to high gear.

A few days later, the timid looking lady with thinning hair, high and near-escaping cheekbones scarping her face directly from an early Hitchcock film advertisement, caught in a landslide of loneliness it was apparent, nodded at my approach. She had been advised of my visit.

"Miss Packard, I am seeking any information I can about a most favorite teacher of mine, Mabel Magnuson. I had her in the seventh grade and I swear I cannot get her out of my mind, though I have not seen her in over sixty years." I paused, thinking to hold back something dear, and then let it all go: "I used to run errands for her from school." I had to make the full course. "A while ago I saw her gravestone at the cemetery. It rushed all these pell-mell years together."

Down the tunnels of eyes of total discomfort I saw the sudden slash of light, and there began without doubt the punctuation of an earnest but slight smile. At first it curved half her lip in a minor distortion, half dragging her mouth into caricature, until she seemed to amass energy to call up the other side; a feeble, forlorn, but full smile that found other lights, other messages, sockets of knowledge bulging their properties.

I had struck home.

A flash from a powerful force passed on her countenance. It might have been the most enlightening look I had ever seen cross a person's face. The timid crow's feet she wore I nearly heard crinkle in their joy, and she offered the slimmest hand ever gestured. "Are you the boy who always went to Mr. Brecht's for her? You are him, aren't you? You're not the boy who wouldn't go that time, are you?" That most serious question flared as strong as the initial flash. There was for one short moment a true association between us, an alignment. The reserve she might have had began to fall away.

With a second breath she answered her own question. "No, you couldn't be." Her eyes rolled over in a halleluiah or Thanksgiving. "No, you couldn't be him. That boy would never come this far to see an old body like this one. God forbid!"

One feeble hand made a feeble passing gesture, a look at the past, a condemnation of that pupil. She looked at me directly and said, in sound conviction, "I will tell you forthrightly, she was one of the loveliest creatures I have ever known. The warmest. The sweetest. The truest. We used to go on vacations together, to some of the grandest places on Earth. I miss her now, as I've missed her since that horrible day." For a rushed moment I saw the same agony flush her face and eyes as had made Mabel Magnuson so remarkably clear at every recall.

"You went on vacations with Miss Magnuson? How marvelous." I was excited. "What places did you go? What was she like as a traveling companion? Did the pain follow her, the kind I saw in the old school when panic hit me broadside. I swear her eyes were dark as an owl's on a dark limb. Like in a dark movie. Times I thought she'd die if I didn't rush out and back until I was out of breath. I'd return from Mr. Brecht's and she'd rush to the girls' bathroom. I was never out of fright that she'd not come back to the classroom."

"Oh, yes," she replied, one hand continually shaking out messages, thinking about what I'd said, measuring it all. "We'd drive separately out of town and leave one of our cars someplace, and then carry on with our most glorious days. Oh, you know how it was then, in those times; the two of us were so sure of ourselves, not caring for the other world of things, touching endlessly, sweetly, never groping. I was beautiful then. I was always beautiful. And her, dear Mabel, until the pain came on her, was the loveliest creature I have ever known. We took in much of Maine on our vacations, high along the coast, often the mountains and a picturesque cabin at a serene lakeside. I'd cook in the morning and wake her, oh, sweet exhausted, lovely Mabel that mountain and sea adored."

I finally had to ask about the other pupil. "Did one boy refuse to go to the druggist?"

The first shot of anger came. "She called on him, for help. Told him what was needed, gave him a note, and that little shit ass of a boy ran right to the principal, shooting off his mouth all the way, telling everybody on the whole first floor what was going on. *Old Razor* Tarkins came straight to Mabel's room and demanded she come to his office. He brought another teacher with him to take over her class. Mabel died in the girls' room a few minutes later, the pain coming as bad as ever, I can imagine, and the stupid asses standing outside the door all caught up in their damn proprieties, heedless of her moans. When they finally did venture into the room, she was dead. I was all the way at the other end of the building. I heard about her. I rushed to her. Razor Tarkins, the truest ass of them all, grabbed my arm, tried to keep me away from her. "I know about you two," he said. I slapped his face. Then I slapped it again. He fired me on the spot, but I didn't care. The most important thing in my life had left me." The wistful look overpowered me, as she closed with, "I have never looked back."

Ethel Packard, so long a survivor of sorts, waved that feeble hand again, saying the visit was over.

Three days later, and two days before she died, I took Ethel Packard for her first visit to Mabel Magnuson's gravesite in more than fifty years. She smiled once and fully, the way I have never seen an old lady smile, and I could hear the crow's feet sending messages in a dialect all their own, something special, something one way toward understanding.

I never found out what took Mabel Magnuson down. It might well have been loneliness of the strangest sort.

In later visits to my comrades, and on the way back down the crooked road, I know Mabel Magnuson's stone heeded my voice, finally released some of its own music for my listening. I'd nod when passing by, wishing her back to the edge of a wide and lonely lake deep in a Maine forest, the silver moon gone to sleep over a far hill, mated loons most serious in their melancholy, and bacon's morning babble calling her from a dreamy sleep.

Too Much Asia to Wipe Off

Chris Banntry yelled, "Who the hell are you? Get off my goddamn bed! This is my goddamn bed! This is my goddamn place!" The soft eyes were looking down at him. His own mouth tasted like shoes. His hip was a real aching bitch, talking down his leg, live as a streamer, a banner jiggling in a wafer breeze. On one leg an itch began its tenure. "Damn ants," he screamed as if promise was a payback. The soft face pulled back abruptly, alarm riding on it, and Banntry swore he smelled fear rising from it, could taste it coming at him as if it were buttered popcorn steeped in the air.

Chris thought he knew where he was.

Sleep in any alley always came piecemeal to Chris Banntry (*and never luck*, he would add, *if anything else*.) He called it *bonesleep* or *curbsleep*, or a number of other things, just as long as minutes of it were sometimes accompanied by a kind darkness. He liked it best where his bones could settle for moments and his mind go blank and his stomach cease its horrible arguments, and the insects, the ants and other crawling enemies, might take a night off from arduous labors. The darkness, inevitably, could bring enemies of all sorts with it, or even the strangest of friends.

That darkness now began its slow descent above him, coming down in the night of the alley. It floated down in pieces, a filtered fog, a shapeless bank of blackness here, a neon fragment there, riding softly over the smells of garbage and dampness and illicit moisture making the alley an outhouse of odors. Here, for sure, gentle reveries and dreams and memories had trouble finding their way home. He thought that all about him was just a piece of Asia away from Asia. Asia, for Chris Banntry, never went away, or never went so far that a look over its shoulder couldn't find him right where he had been, those minutes ago.

The torment of a long-known ache, souvenir of souvenirs, continued its stubborn life at his left hip. Hours before dawn the pain would waken him and say *present,* just as it had all the mornings since he'd first experienced it, jarring any dream of its leaving his body. Darkness was welcomed as well as the smells and the promised moments of ease now descending on him, and he tried not to think about the ants and their swarming tactics, how sometimes the legions of them came in dark resolute waves, ready to take over world, and all the way from Asia.

Red brick and stained mortar and dark gray walls of the alley became brush and thick foliage as he looked at them, as they dimmed at the back scope of his eyeballs. They became his elsewhere. The parts locked in his mind. The fire escape overhead seemed limbs of a perimeter tree, doorways loomed singularly as sentinels, and other forms were other bodies posted in shadow and in shade. A breath of air blew moist-laden. Smells became the old smells: wet, spent gunpowder, acrid, carrying a burnt diesel air in them; flesh smell and flesh rot touched everything; everything came foul. In-country or out-of-country sleep made its approach, coming on, teasing, playing at the edges. His stomach argued again, promised gas as violent as a grenade, then quieted itself, muffled the way Corporal Abersham had shushed a grenade with his body. At the back of his head the block of wood pushed into place humped like a bog man's pillow, making a half promise of softness, tolerating comfort. All it meant was Time, intervening Time, and it all came a clinging grasp of Asia. He dozed off while purple leaves matted into the edge of night and the crawling elsewhere.

Later, but not much at that, he knew he had slept fitfully again, at best. Asia had minimized its presence in the alley. At his hip the ache was saying, *Hey, wake up! I'm still here! You don't get rid of me that friggin' easy!*

He felt hands again, pushing him gently but more fully awake. Under his back the hard reality of cement stated its presence. His nostrils struggled for recognition, and his eyes, and all his senses. Hands pushed again, softly but insistently, not jailer's hands, not top kick's hands, not the hands of an abusive stepfather deep in an Iowa cornfield. Soft hands, but insistent hands.

Dawn, what there was of it to that point, slithered down on him. Clouded in it *was* a face he did not know and a mouth speaking softly, slowly to him. "I'm sorry. I don't mean any harm to you. I just want to help." The hands left his side.

71

Chris Banntry yelled, again, "Who the hell are you?

"I got lost. I wanted to help and I just got lost. I don't know where to go or what to do. I just got lost." The voice was a match for the face, each full of entreaty, bland with dining room ease. Without a doubt, out-of-place this deep in Asia.

"So you get in my bed, in my place. Are you a fag? What the hell you trying to do? I got enough goddamn trouble without you creeping in here." For a moment the reality at his hip was a white pain, blossoming like Willie-Peter out of a detonating shell, reaching out the way petals do in time-delayed films. The contrast was not lost on him.

"I guess the hell you're lost! I guess the hell you don't get to wear that suit out of here either." He felt the quick sense of provincialism rear its head in his threat, a viable threat, one he would never carry out, though he knew its possibilities. His eyes darkened with distrust, his thin lips pursed contemplatively, mockery carried in their curves.

"I don't care about the suit. I just got lost, but I was trying to help. Look," Soft Face said as he reached into his pocket, "I've got some food here. It's just what I could bring now, this time." He spoke as if repeated attempts at such journeys were to be made. From the pocket he withdrew a wrapped packet. "I have sandwiches for you."

"For me?" Chris Banntry said. "How come they're for me? You I've never seen before. What kind are they? D'ja spit in them for a joke?"

"Well, not for you in the beginning, but for someone like you, someone I knew I'd meet here. Well, I suppose you. And I did not spit in them. That's disgusting!" The face hardened a measure. The voice building up breath behind it.

Chris Banntry took the packet. "You didn't say what kind. What are they? Sandwiches gotta have a name. Sweet potato and mustard, whatever, you name them all the time."

The packet loomed thick, wrapped in tin foil. Its edges were neat and trim, the folds square and even, subject to measurement. It had a promising heft. His stomach, he thought, should have been in anxious anticipation, but the grenade sat there, ominous, picking up some of the white heat, some of the

72

Willie Peter. The head of Soft Face relaxed, tipped that knowledge, the mouth opened, the eyes begging acceptance.

Another fookin' do-gooder, Chris thought.

"I made them myself. They're tuna fish. I was going to make roast beef, but I decided not to."

"Why?" Chris said. Slowly he began to peel back the neat edges. They were so neat he felt sacrilegious, as though he were unfolding secrets, hidden ballots.

"Because I was afraid roast beef might be too difficult for chewing." It came a firm and honest answer.

"You make sandwiches for me or one of my buddies and you think we got no goddamn teeth to chew them, like we live on liquids all the time. Drinking it up all the time. You think we're just fookin' trash. You bastards really give me a pain where the sun don't shine." Looking around he added, "And that's not your only problem. Not by a long shot. I bet a dozen guys have already got dibs on your suit." He made it sound like the real threat he had wanted it to be in the first place, a threat as ominous as he could make it.

A rustling sound, paper or cardboard, perhaps coarse cloth, a shifting of one whole surface over another whole surface, emerged out of the alley depths. A cough came as apt as a punctuation mark from deeper in the unknown. Perhaps another sound was a can falling bell-like on edge against stone or the hard edging of a curb, a tinny echo riding free. A piece of daylight touched a brick wall over their heads, a dab of it, morning tilting itself into place for observation, measurement. Chris Banntry let go of Asia as the odor of the tuna fish on rye stuck itself in his nostrils as strong as a bayonet move.

"You're one of them do-gooders, aren't you? Getting social awareness. Getting off on doing one of your nice warm deeds for the day. A pain, man, a real pain. That's what the hell you are, the whole fookin' stinking mess of you. A royal pain in the ever-lovin' ass. City's full of your crap. Up to the ears with it! All out plain fookin' crap!"

Yet rich tuna and rye lifted their bodies into his senses. His stomach fired up again and the battle for survival started anew. Only aromas assailed him, talked him out of voice while he

73

breathed, while Soft Face looked imploringly at him, while the white heat at his hip began its quest of the day, to gain and keep his attention despite what came on the horizon. It's off to a hell of a start, he acknowledged to himself.

"You got a name, sandwich maker?"

"My name is Floyd Spahn." Soft Face tried a weak smile with his name. It did not work.

"You a lefty?"

"No," came the weak reply. "Do I have to be a lefty?"

"I'm jerking you off, man, pulling your chain. He was a Braves pitcher, a lefty, a veteran of the awful wars. My mouth is full of crap and my gut is gonna bust and I had a rotten sleep last night and the goddamn ants are promising to eat me alive and I don't want to eat your fookin' handout. That's just where I'm at for openers."

"What do you live on? What do you eat?" Soft Face had blue eyes and a pony of a nose.

"On handouts, for Christ sakes! Ain't you the fookin' saint of all saints. But I don't paint it all over the headlines. You ask too many questions. My ass is killing me. My leg is killing me. The ants are killing me. My bed's been invaded. The fookin' jungle's like a cobweb all over the place and you want to write a fookin' book. Life sure has its moments, don't it?"

Banntry moved to another sitting position on the cement platform, uttered a string of profanities and moved again. His boots were thin, worn, with leather like that of an old baseball glove worn down by its games, by endless line drives and scooped up grounders carrying playground sand, debris, dust. His pale jeans showed off their chlorine history, faded in spots, holes at the knees, shredded at ankle like straggly whiskers.

"Why'n't you bring Egg fookin' MacMuffin? It's breakfast time, ain't it?"

"I didn't know what to do. I just brought these. It's all messed up with me. I just wanted to help someone sometime. Maybe just one time, I don't know. I don't know why I came here. I just came. I just made the sandwiches and I came down here. I didn't know where I was going and whom I was going to see. I didn't know I was going to see you. I just did it. I did it on my

74

own." The thin jaw set itself a modicum of pride, a sense of accomplishment.

Banntry detected the quick sense of pride in the voice, or accomplishment. Turning his head and looking down the alley, he saw vague light crawling now on the opposite wall as if ivy were growing there on the tiers of bricks. He yelled, "Hey, Morgan!"

A deep-throated voice, megaphonic, James Earl Jones-ish, replied, "What you got there, man?" The voice rose from a shadow lingering yet in another corner, but there was no movement with it.

"What I got here, Morgan, is Beacon Hill Golden Arches come down to visit us."

"I don't mean no goddamn company, man," the voice in the alley said, "I mean what you got there in that hand of yours you goin' to put in that mouth of yours right 'bout now." There was a sense of minor movement, as if a Pacific platelet had shifted.

"Tuna, man, tuna on A-1 fookin' rye. He brought us tuna for breakfast, tuna right off a table on Beacon Hill, tuna with lettuce, tuna with mayo, goddamn tuna without any fookin' coffee."

He turned to Soft Face and the blue eyes and the pony nose. "You got anything else in there, Lefty? Any crap I should be afraid of? That suit ain't for long, you know. You're in Asia now, man. That's a continent of a whole new color!"

"Do you call this Little Asia, then?" Floyd Spahn smiled weakly, an insider's smile being put on, one would think, and then shook his head. "Nothing else. I couldn't do that. I could hardly do this." He gestured about the alley, the stable nothingness, and the darkness still abiding in places, the living threats. His eyes were still full of surprise, as much question in them as one could ask.

Banntry spoke again. "C'mon, Morg. We got us breakfast and no java. Lefty here's got something on his mind, social kind of, *This Living Earth* and whatever comes with it, you know. I guess we're it." He looked at the round face and the blue eyes and the pony nose and the thin hands crossed as if in pose in the lap of the young man sitting beside him. The suit was, even to an untrained eye, very expensive; dark gray, thin lines barely hinting at orange, a cut so neat it might have been painful, like a paper slice on a finger. In the breast pocket a straw, with the paper wrapper still on it, protruded like an afterthought. Banntry looked at the straw the way coaches or teachers elicit responses, his eyebrows raised in demand.

"I was going to bring some milk, but I forgot it. I left too fast. I made the sandwiches and I left too fast." The eyes above the soft mouth and the voice seemed screened, an allowed opaqueness in residence. There was an almost doll-like quality pervading them, too fashioned, too temperate, the mild reserves barely touched. A dim light glowed somewhere in the body of them, as if only the parking lights were on. In the poor light, in the glimmer of the false dawn, the face was nearly apathetic, a moon of paled, ashen ivory full of nothing but apology, calculated meekness. Banntry had seen a thousand and one faces like it. He had never counted on them for anything, ever.

The rustling sound came again from the alley, from the shadow in a far corner, out of which walked a shadow of a tall black man in a long black coat.

"Tuna," said the tall newcomer. "I'll be damned. Tuna on rye, and for breakfast. Ain't we something' today. Ain't we somethin' special. Beacon Hill tuna on rye. Ain't that A-fuckin' well. I ain't sure what lunch is goin' to brin', but I can tell you I can hardly wait none." He stretched one hand toward Banntry. "Like I tole you last night, your lucky day comin' up wit' the sun this mornin'. Ain't no way around it, Chris. You got some luck comin' on you today."

His huge hand wrapped around a sandwich. "You got stars in the right attitude. They been gettin' closer for you all week. You gettin' shit lucky for a change. Did you tell him about his suit?" He looked directly at Banntry and then at the mild speaker, the evidence of threat unmistakably carried in his voice. "Them stars is different. Collision course for sure! Some thin's just can't be helped." He bit and chewed and shrugged almost in one motion.

Chris Banntry bit into his sandwich. His teeth felt wired, his jaw felt tired. Out of practice, he thought. In a quick motion he brushed an ant off the backside of one hand and screamed another long string of profanities, picturing the world as a huge crawled-on-all-over dung ball.

The tall man in the black coat laughed loudly, the sounds rattling both in his throat and in the corners of the alley, guttural and somehow imperfect in their tone. "They's better than worms, Chris. At least you can brush them off. When the worms get aholt of you, they own you for good and then some. It's like plowin' wit' them. Just turn everythin' over, right down to bone. Leave nothin' but bone, like rocks in a dark field, skulls and empty sockets and leg bones and arms spilt all over creation, the way the good lord meant it to all end up. We's just meat so's the world can carry on without us when we go spoilin'. They's call it legacy."

Chris Banntry chewed and swallowed and chewed some more. The range of his whole jaw felt better and the grenade in his stomach lay pinned for the moment.

He motioned toward the gift bringer. "Thank you, Lefty, for the tuna. Morg here is probably goin' to carry on for hours if we let him. Morning exercise or something like that. Give him an inch and he'll take all your rope. Some guys call him Preacher. What I should do is call him late for tuna on rye. But he's right, and so am I, about your suit. It's a stick-out down here. Keep half a dozen guys drunk a whole week if they wanted."

"I wouldn't care if it were taken from me, as long as they gave me something else to wear." The fear had left his voice. He stood up, as short as he was a bit taller than he was. "I have other suits. I could give them some, but not so as they could drink all week. That's not a fair exchange. It's not what I meant to do. Every day I feel useless. I keep thinking about all of this. It frightens me, just having everything right at hand. I've done nothing all my life, really nothing, and it frightens me. When I go I want to know I've done something for somebody else, for other people. My whole life has been a waste. I don't do anything for anybody. When I'm trying to sleep at night, when all I can do is measure things, it hurts. It makes the night longer than it ought to be."

His jaw hung slacker, his shoulders sagged.

Morgan said, "How much you like it where the sun don't shine, Lefty?" His laughter followed like a bad echo.

The small body of the man shook out his response. "I'm not a gay, but I knew it would be like this. You think I'm just a joke, that I don't count for anything. You think I want attention for this or something else just as horrible. Well, you're wrong!" Light had lifted much of the shadow off him. Banntry saw there really was a bit of orange swimming in the lines of the suit, and the cut of the cloth *was* severe enough to have caused pain. Hair on the young man was razor clean, lines of the cut as severe as the suit had been cut. For a moment he thought the morning visitor might have been stamped out by a sheet metal die. Other copies of him were all around the city, hundreds of them, thousands of them, pressed from the same die, the same inordinate and clumsy power coming to bear to produce a mere echo, a flimsy sheet metal robot turned out for a quick spin around the old city. He snickered, "Casual is as casual does," to himself.

"What's down there?" Floyd Spahn said, tossing his head in the direction of the alley, a bit of dare riding on him like a meek metaphor, frail but seated in place.

"That's Asia down there, Lefty. You don't want to go too deep into Asia. Some time if you go too deep there's no way to get rid of it. There's leaves there big as a man's shadow. Time sucked right up into all the roots. Claims in the air strong as birthmarks. It don't just let go sometimes! I don't just mean Hong Kong and Nippon and all their crap made out of plastic and cut glass and fookin' shiny tin. There's more than junk and jungle and islands and peninsulas. Asia hangs on too fookin' long for most people. It's a leech if there ever was one, and that's an early warning for you, if you can let yourself hear it."

"You said I shouldn't have come here, but I'm doing all right, aren't I? Now you're telling me not to go down there. You're eating my sandwiches and I appreciate that. It's something I had to do and there are other things I have yet to do. You'll have to try to understand me. I am not afraid. I came here, didn't I? There is something special in all of this you might never understand."

He stood up and the lines of the suit seemed straighter, and the light reflecting in his eyes fixed them with a faraway look, almost dreamy. He walked off into the lingering shadows of the alley. They swallowed him wholly and quickly.

Moments later there was a muffled noise in the alley, in the darkness that had not let go, a darkness half a world away. It sounded as if a sewer had been flushed or a sump hole drained. Then there was silence and air breathing on itself and light trying to find its way home.

"What was that?" Morgan said, craning his head perfunctorily.

"That," Chris Banntry said, "that's probably the end of Lefty's Delicatessen."

"Or Lefty's Haberdashery," Morgan added, over the remnants of tuna on rye and mayo against the back of his teeth as pure as oil, and daylight still lifting shadows from their places of rest.

Keepsake

Coming off the ice at the lonely end of the Rapid Tucker's Pond, his feet starting to numb in earnest, the new snow like razor blades on his face, Bannock "Brace" Bannon was compelled to look behind him, across the pond closing down fast in white fury. Earlier he had seen the girl in the comely figure swing around the edge of the pond, admiring her ease, her grace on the blades, her hair at times flying out as straight as a windy pennant.

One impulse hit him that she was a stranger, not because he hadn't seen her before, but because she was perilously close to the channel between the two islands of Rapid Tucker's Pond. In the ten years he had been here at the far end of the pond, a loner in an old cabin that took an endless amount of maintenance, the channel had been frozen only once, and that back in his first year, the worst year of all. Was all that decision time and tempest here again, coming down on top of him anew? The raw intelligence of his place in life was coming with its onerous beat. Was this girl sent to test him again, give him another chance? Make amends?

Was it worth it? He had, with all his conviction, tried to help that other girl. Blew it all to Hell he did. To Hell and back!

Now that knowledge jumped at him, and it had a fire to it. A buzz. A bell ringer. All this time, away from the harsh reality of the world, he had been reclusive and somewhat happy; free of much of the duress and torment he had gone through after the other incident. God, he marveled, how could he reduce it after all this time to an incident? He had made up a whole history, had invented Brace Bannon to take the place in this world of Halvor Gustafson, M.D., stripped of his rights because of that one abortion mishap. On many occasions he had called himself a "runaway," so often that the tag no longer hurt. It went along with "incident," it seemed. He could ignore all its attachments most of the time. It was only in darkness that it kept the pain alive, below the surface, in the stream of his life.

But now he could not ignore this girl, test or no test, chance or no chance. Better go back out there and at least advise her of the dangers, he said to himself, even as the numbness came into his toes dull as forgotten chilblains. Slight of build, little body fat because of his routine and regimen, but a skater for ten years, he started out across the pond, staring feebly through the blinding snow. The responsibility fell to him and only him, the nearest house at least five hundred yards away down the far shore, all obliterated by the squall. If he did nothing, his conscience, in the dark hours, would haunt him.

Leaning into the storm, he raked his eyes against the low clouds of snow, swirling, the barriers shifting. Nothing formulated or contoured came to his eyes. No edges. No shadow line. No being. Perhaps, he thought, that was a single sound he had just heard, but one he could not identify. Heading to the point where he had last seen the girl, he guessed her to be about twenty-four or -five. When the wind died momentarily, the ice looking like a linen sheet on a huge bed, he saw nothing. Thinking she had obeyed the threat of the elements, he turned to go home. Again he thought about the channel, about his dark and lonely hours, the girl from long ago still making an impact deep inside. Sometimes the worst terror was not remembering her name. I'm it, he said, thinking again of this new girl skating alone. One look won't hurt.

An acute awareness hit him that he was being commandeered, impelled, magnetized; it was a scrutable sensation gnawing within him. It was assuming shape.

The ice was broken and it was getting dark. A darker shadow floated in the dread water of the channel. She had been wearing dark blue. This was a deeper blue. Getting closer, hearing the ice crack underneath him and the thunder of its plate-shifting danger, he stumbled on a discarded hockey stick and instinctively grabbed it. Another look and he was positive the girl was in the water, face down and motionless.

My god, he thought, it's only been a few minutes. The ice roared again, the platelets shifted again, the rolling crack near thunder ran under his feet one more time. Not being the best swimmer, the skates would certainly drag him down. He was mouthing words to himself: Do not rush this. We both must stay alive. Be careful. Lie down. Inch your way out. Get hold of her. There's only you. Nobody knows we are here. We are alone. We are all alone. The words were ratcheted in his head, coming back, coming back.

The pain in his feet had disappeared, but he could feel the weight of each skate. Suddenly he was cold. Was it fear? Was he wet? Could he get them both back to his cabin? Would the fire be warm enough? Was she still alive? It had been mere minutes.

The ice held up. His hand, icy and freezing, a numbness beginning to be a pain in its own right, caught at her hood. Lying across the broken hockey stick (bless the boy who had left it) he pulled her onto the ice with considerable difficulty. She had to be maneuvered onto a safer, thicker surface. She was heavy, wet, probably not breathing well, if at all. Into her mouth he breathed, into that cold but luscious mouth, upon that beautiful face now creased and plagued by the freezing water, her eye sockets like pearls of ice. Again and again he breathed and pushed into her stomach and breathed and jostled the soggy and inert body, until the sudden flush of water gushed from her mouth and a breath of shattering cold air was called down into her lungs.

Oh, he was thankful for his long hours of skating, the hours he chopped wood and stacked it and carried it into the cabin and was warmed by it half a dozen times, and the long and demanding walks he took into the deeper part of the forest, away from the prying eyes. His body, with the girl now an adjunct to it, now an extension, made serious demands on his energy and determination. Somehow, he must get her to the cabin, get her warm, minister to her. The idea of ministering to a needy soul overwhelmed him; he had been there before, and it had all been too clumsy.

It took him nearly twenty minutes to get her to the small porch of the cabin, newly formed thin ice coming on her like lace. Walking the last thirty feet on his blades, hitting rocks along the way, he knew they'd be no good for skating for a while. The picture of hidden sparks came to him, flint being struck by the good steel down in the snow. Near exhaustion, feet loaded with chilblains, hands so fiery yet numb, he finally got her inside the rude and clumsy cabin, and onto the bed.

First he stripped off his parka, then worked on her clothing, cutting her out of her jacket and pants, getting the skates off her feet, using a razor blade to cut her laces. It was the blade edge that triggered him, invasive and yet so superficial. That other and older terror came back again; that young girl, also lovely, so young, who had come to him for help, cut off from her family, alone, at the edge of hysterics he had not known, only to be buried under them in one quick pass over his soul.

He pulled her sweater over her head, ripped off the wet blouse, unsnapped her bra, and pulled her underpants off. In her near deadly state he was suddenly aware of how lovely she was. Before he tucked a woolen blanket about her he took one look along the length of her body. She was a most marvelous young woman; her breasts were lovely and full and the aureoles, surely and naturally almost a burnt orange, closed now on a purple flush. He thought he should rub them, but he refrained. Not in ten years had he seen a woman nude, or touched one. No patients. No lovers. No nightly visitor from the nearby town. There was a moment of exhilaration when he swore a perfume was loose in the cabin. The shock of hair at her midsection grasped at his eyes. In spite of the cold and the snow and the sweat now rising about him, his mouth had gone dry. His throat was dry with a sudden need, a strange and forgotten yielding coming at him out of his past.

There it was, the saline lovely aroma of the Rumney Marsh where the tide moved its moon madness. That's what came to him now, in the middle of a winter storm. Saline, salty marsh, old territories. Musk of ever. The girl exuding self, the essence of such being long unknown to him.

The folds of the blanket went around her almost sensually. If he wanted to he knew he could assess her curves, her loveliness, and the soft and disparate masses of her graces. A beautiful range to her hips showed itself. It made the back of his throat hurt. Chilblains at last had left his hands. Moments later the single bulb overhead went out and he knew the electric line had gone down again and might be hours before it was restored. He had no phone. They would be alone for the duration of the storm at least.

The fire in the old wood stove was small but alive and he added two logs after a quick feed of kindling. The flames leaped in moments, and she breathed slowly but evenly. He stripped his own wet clothes off. The kettle of water on the back of the wood stove began to simmer when he moved it to the middle of the stovetop.

From one shelf of the cabinet he took a can of soup, opened it and placed it on the stove, adding a can of water. Only later did he know it was celery soup, the room filling with the odor, sharing it with the smell of the young woman collapsed under his blanket, her breathing even at last, as if she were asleep. Celery and the odor of the young woman came on him, the rich saline spread of the Rumneys, full and pungent, making him take a deep breath so that he could recognize all the ingredients; all his hungers came on him; all his past came on him. He remembered the girl who had died from the perilous abortion. Whole scenes, ten years in the past, came looping out of dark corners, bringing his life back into the room.

For three hours he watched her, leaving once to get wood off the porch pile, going once to the makeshift john off the end of the porch, the snow still coming down, somewhere along the edge of the pond the power lines down under a fallen limb or a blow-down too tired to hang on through another storm. In the midst of the whiteness the darkness of the storm threatened its severity, and made for a long promise.

When she woke, stirred uneasily, realizing she was naked beneath the blanket, looking about for her clothes, seeing a strange man across a strange room, it appeared her mishap came back to her in a rush. She began to tremble, inhaled excitedly, almost hyperventilated. The blanket was pulled tightly around her throat. Her eyes scanned the rudeness of the room, saw the flicker of the fire through an open grating of the stove, seemed to assess her whole situation, and then nodded at Brace Bannon. "You pulled me out?" she said, her voice soft, firm, not filled with anxiety, fear, or too much surprise. "I could hear the ice creaking underneath me. I tried to get away, but I broke through. My clothes and skates pulled at me. I remember seeing you, how smoothly you skated. I wondered if you were alone." A shiver ran through her. "I don't know what happened next."

"I'm a doctor, young lady, so don't worry. I had to get you out of the water and off the ice and out of those clothes." The flush was on his face. He could feel it; and knew she could see it, even with the lights out and a single candle burning on a shelf. "Are you hungry? I have some hot soup. There's coffee on the stove. I can make something heavier for you, decent, more nourishing." He managed to keep up a pattern of chatter, his face still flushed,

84

her eyes still on him. "But I'm afraid we're here for a spell. The power lines are obviously down again. Happens all the time. I'm the only one at this end of the pond. Almost half a mile out in the lonely." His head shook as if punctuating the last sentence. "Not worth a whole lot to the power company." He stood up and put his hand out. "My name is Brace Bannon. I used to be a doctor. I messed up once and I've been here, out of action, out of the limelight, for about ten years now. It suits me, here. I have been fairly comfortable. It's pleasant most of the time in spite of all this." He fanned his hand out as if to introduce her to crudeness, bare necessities, solitude, and the storm beating at the small cabin. His nod said he believed she understood his feelings. No assurance came to him that she could possibly understand the pain and suffering that had overpowered him. He had long believed few people could ever know; his whole belief system had been corrupted. This day, even minimally, had brought some kind of amends. There was, however, a great lingering fear that he would screw it up before the day was over.

The girl sat up on the bed, the soft blanket at her throat, under her chin. Part of one leg, one thigh, showed its whiteness in elegance, a graceful curve to the width of it, a most lovely thickness. Brace Bannon's eyes caught the flash of white, the full curve, the inveterate promise. She caught his eyes and it was as if she was saying, "Did you look at me when you took my clothes off? "No other message on her face or in her voice. "My name is Devahn Nesting. I think my mother was trying to play some kind of game between me and my father. I don't like him very much. My mother doesn't either. I think he had several girlfriends, probably right in his office. I'm their only common ground. He's filthy rich; she's a lonely middle-age witch bent on some kind of retribution, hassling, or evil. I'm not sure which, but I got tired of it the whole mess. I was running away from it all."

"Are you warm enough?" Brace Bannon said. The top of the stove had passed from dull red back to a cooler black. The wind humped at the door. Her legs hung below the bottom of the blanket. A light redness touched at her toenails, as pink as it was red, and he wondered if it might have matched the lipstick she must have been wearing earlier.

"Would you have any pajamas? I can't sleep without pajamas." She looked down on the bed, as if the die was already cast. The toes on one foot wiggled slightly, as if it were an expression of something she had forgotten.

Once, long ago, he recalled, there had been body music and body language. "I have extra long johns, tops and bottoms, plenty of sweaters, a couple of sweat shirts I've never worn." A shrug crossed his shoulders. "I don't have any pajamas."

"I'll take long john bottoms, a pair of socks and a sweat shirt, if you can spare them. If I'm to be here for a while I might as well be warmer than I am right now." She looked at the pan of soup on the stove.

Brace poured a small bowl for her and pulled a box of saltines out of a breadbox hung on the wall. "I think it's celery soup. I'm not sure. I lost the label. It's hot." The soup and crackers were set on a small end table. "I'll get you the clothes."

He could hear her at the soup and the crackers, eating as if she relished every swallow. "God, this is good. I don't know if I ever had celery soup." He blushed again, knowing instantly that she was not naïve or innocent. He turned around, away from her, so she could dress, and he heard the rustle of clothes.

At the closure of sound, Brace Bannon turned to see the naked loveliness of Devahn Nesting. The bubble of breath caught itself in his throat. She was about the loveliest thing he had ever seen. It had been lifetime-long since he had seen such a vision. The legs were fantastic, the full and shapely breasts were eyefuls, the span of hips demanded attention, her eyes wide and strangely warm had separate speech in them.

"You might as well look again. I want to see what's on your face when you look at me. I'm not a virgin; I've done it with boys I liked, who knew what they were up to. I don't like malingerers or pawers who don't know what they're supposed to do for a woman. I don't want to get pregnant right now. Not for a couple of years."

She sat down and slipped the elegant legs into the long john bottoms and pulled them up when she stood. The sweatshirt, with a bit of hassle, fell over her gorgeous breasts. The socks she put on last. The vision of her remained in place. Above the celery

soup aroma, something from her rode the air, came across the
small room in an absolute hurry to get to him. Earlier, on a
summer eve he had slipped into Rumney marsh and went looking
for Little Sandy, a swimming hole he had heard about. There'd
been talk of horseshoe crabs with spiked horns, but what still
lingered was the smell of the marsh, the saline-rich warmth as the
tide eased out through the many small canals that laced the grid-
work of a marsh. It was warmly potent even now.

"Oh," she added, "I'm in no rush to get home. They don't
know where I am anyway." Back to the soup she went, and the last
of the saltines. Her eyes were wide and warmer yet, her voice
almost a riddle in itself, when she said, "Would you have a beer?"

The suggested idea of a full-fledged cheeseburger brought
her back to other needs. Brace put a couple of them together, as
the stove kept the room warm, as the storm continued to beat on
outside, and her heady aromas were at last suffused by cheese
overlapping the hamburger patties, getting cooked in a bit of fat.
They finished off the three beers he had been saving.

Later, after hours of talking, a new candle lit, the stove fed
a few times and set up for the night, Devahn Nesting said, "I am
getting tired now. I know we have to share the bed. Don't worry,
it's okay by me. You did me a great service today. I am very
grateful, but I am very tired. You are a marvelous skater. I was
watching you, in case you didn't know, that long easy stride you
have." She slipped under the blanket and rolled over. She went to
sleep quickly.

The candle flickered a kind of angelic light across her face.
Lashes, about as long as they can get, flared from her lids. Her
lips, he thought, were perfect. Even in sleep, they were perfect;
slight pout, curved miraculously, yet ready for speech. He was not
sure if they were red or redder, but they were perfect, and he
thought of old signs of red lips, how they advertised status and
condition, sent off signals. The thought told him he was still able
to measure impact, that he was still a man, that his genes were still
in place, that capability was still here. Then, as the candle itself
began to show signs of failing, he slipped in beside her, inhaled
the same aroma that had crossed the room to him all night, thought
of lost successes, remembered a girl once in a car outside a

package store on the way to the outdoor theater, who had taken off her girdle while he was in the store. He remembered the light in her eyes, the sound of her voice when she said, "You would have gotten it off soon enough." When he last closed his eyes he remembered how her skirt rode up on the glory of her thighs as he purchased their tickets at the ticket booth, the ticket seller looking down into the car, wide-eyed, nodding.

Some hours later he woke. Devahn Nesting was stroking him lightly, her head resting on his chest. "Has it really been ten years?" He could not see her eyes. Her hand was full of fire, yet was almost a phantom touch. From under the blanket she assailed him again, the essence of her being wafting up under his chin, finding knowledge in him, bringing knowledge. In his chest his breath caught at itself, and old knowledge, old territories, came back in a rush. At first the girl at the outdoor theater flooded him with memories and odors and a touch he suddenly realized had not ever gone away. Then this nearly drowned girl, this girl who drank his beer, this girl who suffused this old cabin as it had never been suffused, said, "It's going to be my treat."

Those magnificent and lovely lips encircled him. He began to cry softly. She said, "Cry all you want. I'm here all night. And I'll stay as long as you want me to."

The girl in the car at the outdoor theater finally drove away in the storm, down the shore of the pond, out of sight forever. The frightened girl of the abortion fled with her. Once more he heard the sound of the ice cracking under his feet out on the pond, out where the channel always made noises. Part of his life seemed to move the way the pond ice moved, immense, lethargic but so powerful, like glaciers, like ice sleds out of the millennium. Where he had been summoned again to do good, he knew with certainty that he was now being awakened from a long sense of pretense.

Then there was silence and darkness and a sweet aroma hanging folds about his head, the warmth of Rumney Marsh thick with life and growth and an essence of life where it all began, at the edge of the eternal sea.

Fourth of July Homecoming

The old mill had given off odd sounds since the day it closed down. Now it gave off a sense of passage.

All the way back to the last Fourth of July the boys had saved a cache of fireworks, the three pals, Snag and Chris and Charlie B, all twelve years old within three days of each other. "Pals to the end," they had said, squirreling away the fireworks in Snag's Aunt Lil's barn leaning away from one century and into another. And many times those same hidden articles promised to smoke and explode from their secret hideaway, the boys' want for noise and excitement so strong at times, at times like hunger tantrums. But they had saved them for a special occasion. "Promise made is promise kept," Snag had said on Veterans' Day, his voice hard as wire, though the tantrum pummeled alive in his gut.

So Snag and Chris and Charlie B came together on the specially appointed night, the national holiday, and crept up on the backside of the Old Scott's Mill, closed tight as an angry man's fist, sitting there beside the old, slow Saugus River. It was a mill as marked as time itself, whose existence seemed to transcend the town and its beginnings. Now and then it became a shell of nacre the way an early bronze moon could make it eerie and distant and out of this world. It was a piece of another time, another dimension, for none of them could begin to imagine the gallons of workers' sweat that had seeped into the floors of the structure for parts of two centuries.

One box and two bags of choice explosives, stashed away for ninety slow-as-snails days, figured in their arms as something Fort Sumter or another historic battle site might have loosed. Tonight there'd be a new war on the silence gripping the old mill, on the monstrous darkness that moonless nights allowed to cling to the mill, and on whatever lurked in it or around it.

Lighting their sticks of punk they stood on the bank of the river and the smell coasted thickly in the night as if an old barn had been turned inside out. Once, earlier, Chris had explained that his grandfather affirmed that punk was made from camel dung. Each of them inhaled the acrid and known and nostalgic smell as it

89

fingered memories of past celebrations filled with "oohs," and "ahs," and "ohs."

All their memories said time was eternal, spilled on a level coming to them and moving away from them, but tonight disruption was their game. Disruption and noise and affirmation of the minor manhood working its endless way down in their genes.

The Saugus River ran away at the foot of the huge red brick building, the calm waters swishing slowly against the cluttered rock dam site at the foot of the red brick building. Above them, ranging out of the trees, darkness still came plodding on, the near silence moving across their skins asking to be known. Snag's Aunt Lil once had said darkness came on like a beggar man to close the end of day.

"It's only brick," Snag said, his natural spirit bucking up his current assessment. His hand touched the side of the mill, its doors now closed for as long as they had been alive; a monolithic, ghostly creature of a building, windows boarded up, doors frozen in place with huge spikes; eyes that could not see, mouths that could not speak. There was, however, something else in the touch of that stone, something mossy, something growing, something without a voice, but threatening.

They had known forever that it was there.

Snag, as fearsome as any boy they knew, could feel the presence of something if only in the touch of the stone. Creatured, but not quite visible; it might not breathe, but it was there. Yet no one, none of their friends or neighbors, had ever been hurt. It was what they had counted on, in its own perilous argument.

"Yuh," Chris said, feeling the fuzz on the back of his neck with a threat of electricity in it, "So how come they see a glow of flames every Fourth of July. At midnight. From the only window that's not boarded up. The one way up in the peak out front? Tell me how that gets done. All the floors have been taken out. The whole place is nothing but a shell. So how come so many people have seen a red glow in that window way up there? Even my father said he saw it, expected the place was about to burn down." His twelve year old face was squeezed into his own questions, his mouth still pursed, his chin and that pursed mouth still asking for an explanation. The three of them were always blue-eyed; now, at

90

this juncture, they were dark-eyed.

Snag bristled as only Snag could be bristled, the tooth of his name prominent, his jaw prominent, his eyes steely, his breath measured. "How should I know?" he said. "I ain't been in there. I ain't seen anybody go in or come out, ever. Maybe it's like a captured Aurora Borealis, like it was caught in there the very first time it was locked up. Something crazy, like that. Or a bum gets in there every year to play tricks on us. Like having his own routine. But we promised we'd light it up one way or another. And I'm all for getting inside somehow, anyhow. Maybe plopping off one of the plywood boards over the windows. We all promised." He was standing tall, asserting some kind of authority that prior bravery and recklessness had granted him.

"I didn't say anything about not doing it. I'm not yellow!" Chris was breathing heavy as he spoke. And the darkness deepened and a small breath of a wind stirred in the near leafless trees and Charlie B froze straight up as he heard a soft moan come out of that small breath of air. It rode over the thick smell of the burning punk.

"We're not alone," he said, his hand gripping Snag's arm so hard his fingernails dug into the camouflaged material of Snag's fatigue jacket.

"It's the wind, Charlie," Snag said. "Nothing to it. Just the wind. It's a midnight wind. Aunt Lil says every the wind around here has its own voice."

And then, right then on that night, at or near the stroke of midnight, as if commanded by a presence, an omnipotence, the plywood cover over a peaked window high above their heads pulled away from the window frame with the shriek of nails being yanked. It fell and smashed on the rocks below.

The boys froze in place, their breaths caught between sound and no sound. And the yearly and eerie light came at last from that high window, a red moving glow the way flames lick at campfire wood. Slow. Sultry. Expectant. Then it came a sudden blue glow, then a red glow and a green glow. And the moan came again, and faint and distant music trooped in with it as if drums and fifes were playing on the side of Vinegar Hill and were bouncing off the mill's walls, and firelight swept against the high window like a new fire banked in a furnace. It was music and it was but a step up from silence, and it was so light, so distant, so feathery, so winged, it might not have been. Now, it said in an unspoken voice. The boys were not sure of anything.

Charlie B dropped his bag of fireworks, his in-taken breath merely a small echo riding his body. Right down to his new sneakers he shook. Chris held his box as if it were his last bullet. Some thing was standing against them in the night and they must protect themselves. Snag, jawboned Snag, expeditionary leader, his nerves cut and frayed only a bit, from his glowing punk lit and heaved a long-wicked 2-inch salute at the nearest plywood window.

"There!" he said. "There!" The enemy to be accosted and surmounted.

The explosion ripped into the silence, and the sudden flare of light lit the hooded window and disappeared just as quickly as it had come. The overhead light leaped again, the window suddenly alive in red and blue and then an orange glow. Drums, old drums, beat somewhere, an old tattoo of drums, a line of drums in a long forgotten parade, a rolling echo from a lost or glorious battle. At first they believed the drums came from Vinegar Hill, and then they realized that they came from inside the old mill itself, off the walls, and fifes came slowly with the drums, and the flames glowed brighter in the high window. And a discipline, each one noticed, seemed to come with the drums and the fifes, a unity, regulated though faint, as if under orders.

And then, with a sudden and profound silence, the light went out. Darkness fell again, more than a beggar this time; a dense darkness full of time and lineal pursuits, a darkness of summonses and declarations from an insurmountable place, a darkness that reached out to touch the three boys. They shivered in anticipation more than fear. They were present at something unknown but pronounceable, ghostly but real. From Vinegar Hill again it seemed to come, the faint and distant call of mystic notes riding an unknowing wind, riding a brief thermal the eye never sees; intelligent notes, bugle notes, timeless notes.

Snag leaped from his kneeling position. "Listen!" he commanded, his voice stern, demanding, the barking voice of an infantry line sergeant. "Listen!"

Overhead the red glow came back in the high round window near the peak of the old mill. And the notes sounded clear and distinct. And they came from inside the mill, not from the outside, but from inside old Scott's Mill.

Those were timeless notes coming at them.

With messages in them.

Charlie B and Chris reached for minute recognition of the notes, but it was Snag who knew them. "That's Assembly that's playing. I heard it on Tim's web site. That's Assembly. I heard it on a web site. I downloaded a whole mess of them, but that's Assembly." In his voice was heard a definite change, as though he might have snapped to attention in the ranks.

Mesmerized, they heard more bugle calls, some Snag knew and some he didn't. He was not flustered. "Call to Arms," he said proudly, listening again, nodding his head, "and Boots and Saddles" a few moments later, and then, still distant notes coming to them, "First Call," and "Call to Quarters," and finally, the sounds now down inside them, touching at their souls, standing at attention in the dark, he said in that deepening voice, "To the Colors."

Their blood froze. They were rapt and enraptured, transplanted but in place, something crying to get out of them, to have a voice of its own. Each of them felt it in their own way, yet somehow acknowledged the sharing.

The door of old Scott's Mill popped open right beside them, and the faint and still far-reaching notes came to them, and horse hooves tromping on hard ground and the clumping of hundreds and hundreds of boots on packed gravel. The boys looked inside, amazed, frightened, and a line of horse troops, gray and blue cavalry, passed in review, eyes-righting them, moving past them in formation. Others came clothed in a dozen or so different uniforms, Johnny Reb gray, Yankee blue, Army O.D., airman's blue and sailor blue, dress Marine and fatigue Marine, war on top of endless war, time on top of immemorial time. They were an illustration of all wars, and all losses, and the ranks were thick and heavy and dense with the souls of innumerable warriors.

From a post in the ranks, well back in the ranks, a deep and resonant voice came to them. "We're coming home, boys. We're coming home and we don't have to go off anywhere anymore. Not this night. Not ever. We're all the ones who never came home, but we've been waiting for you. We've tried every Fourth of July for years. It's only on the Fourth that we can come home."

From a limitless distance, evoked and called at one side of the mill's interior, they came, a long endless march of men, shoulders back, heads up, coming home after their own eternity; Gettysburg, Stone Mountain, San Juan, Chateau Thierry, Omaha Beach, Kwajalein, Chosin Reservoir, Heartbreak Ridge, Dak To, deserts and jungles too numerous to mention, all the odd points of the fiery Earth, and all the harsh graves of that eternity.

"Eyes right," the deep voice said, commanding, and then, as if stating a memorial of their own kind, added, "We did it for the young un's and for the old-timers, too."

Snag stood as tall as he'd ever stand. He motioned his comrades to attention as new notes came on the thin, cool air. "Retreat," he whispered, the huskiness suddenly at home in his voice, arrived manhood in his voice, spine upright, nerves in place. "That's Retreat," he said again, his voice still deeper, resonant. The somber notes carried for long moments and the line of troops and horsemen stood at attention, just the way Snag and his pals stood.

And then, more distant than any call ever heard before or ever afterward, out of a summer darkness, the smell of burning punk as acrid as spent gunpowder crawling in the air, a lone bugle's notes came riding another feathery and light thermal from the very ends of time.

"You'll not forget this night, will you, boys?" And the deep voice was gone and the troopers were gone and the horsemen were gone, and the lights drifted off to night again, and a single and momentary note from a still more distant bugle hung itself on the pinnacle of air as Taps ended the most memorable holiday of all time.

Sneaker on the Beach

Jadon Calix was complex and complete, yet here he was with simple dawn playing him like strings on a violin, teasing him out and about in the universe, along with a godforsaken, obviously stinking, lone *Adidas* sneaker. In one particularly bright shaft of light, perhaps a mental shaft he later confessed, he had seen the single sneaker on the beach, harsh as an old idea left behind to ferment for itself. The toes of the sneaker faced the sea, as if the supposed late owner had been at departure, or at contemplation most sincere.

Jadon Calix loved the beach in the morning, especially when the Gulf was quiet. He'd been up much of the night, knowing that in a few days he'd have to leave Louisiana and head back north. Two months hardly seemed enough, yet he would have to leave. The generosity of the Bredens had been overwhelming. Their son Paul had been his comrade, had died in his arms right out on the Iraqi desert. He had been able to tell Paul's parents how it all happened, down to Paul's last words. "Find my Louisiana, Jadon, you'll love it."

Jadon Calix loved the endless beach because he had known terror on the desert. Though that desert was halfway around the world, it was too recent to forget. Amazement overpowered him when he realized sand was the one constant in both lonely places. Now, with the sand compact under his feet, not shifting between tides like odds in a betting parlor, or boats hooked by hawsers out on the Gulf, he fully contemplated the differences of the sandy geographies.

An inner message told him the day itself was different too. Earlier, much earlier, the sun had come on slowly, like a surprise was at hand. The rim of the sea, at the eastern horizon, bloomed the way a new orchid comes, first purple and then an orange-purple and then, in an attempt at utter beauty, a slow gracious lavender, as if evening had taken the place of dawn. It crept up on Jadon, and then, like a sudden change of mind, it banged him right between the eyes when he saw the lone sneaker practically haloed.

His handsome face erupted with intrigue. That face bore a solid chin and a happy smile, a kind of opponent of that solid chin.

He had deep eyes that both sought and delivered messages in quick instances, the blond head often tilted with curiosity telegraphing its existence. Mrs. Breden, the day he came knocking at their door, saw the most attractive young man on the porch from one of her windows, telling her husband, "I swear this is Paul's friend, Jadon Calix. He's about the handsomest man I've ever seen, with all due apologies, my dear, a few years removed." She chuckled immediately, knowing he would somehow bring some new life back into their darkened lives. They rushed him into their home with a gracious welcome and thanks.

Now, on the beach, the combers coming slowly, he wondered if the sneaker belonged to a one-legged, one-footed beachcomber. He laughed lightly at himself, dawn rosy with him, sharing its outlook and full prism. It was worth wondering, he confirmed, his mind leaping around and about, getting himself shifted here and there purposefully. Did such a one-legged man play the drums? The piano? Gamble? Tap time with one foot? Show impatience? Share shots and beers? Bull his way in bed in spite of an infirmity?

Three or four more times that morning, gulls calling, air sweet and salty at the same time as he walked up and down the beach, eyeing rounded stones, collecting glass particles worn smooth by the ocean's play, kicking remnants and other shards of life, he passed by the sneaker, still outbound it appeared. Though it was somewhat worn, beat up in whatever game it might have been at in its days, he knew at one time it must have been one of the gaudy, outspoken types, styling at least for all it was worth and at a hundred and twenty bucks a pair. Times change, he argued.

Jadon could not call back all the nights when Paul's words came down upon him again like a message out of the sky, from far off, the tone of his voice thin and narrow and weak, as if escaping from a star wobbling on the horizon. Much of it haunted him as a task left undone, a promise not kept. Never then could he go back to sleep, Jadon's other messages coming back also, the way one memory sharpens another, hones it into shape, grabs on for all of dear life, not willing to let go. Often he thought it was like knowing barbed wire in the dark.

Another statement of Paul's kept coming back; the time when they were in a reserve area, the weapons out of hand, the stars promising difference, an edge of a breeze without sand in it loose as blades. "There's so much adventure there, Jadon. Don't miss out on it. Between the Gulf and the bayous there's a whole lot of crawl space. Find some of it. I did. I loved it. You will too."

That probably started it off, a simple reaction one splendid morning when Paul wouldn't let go. He got up early, after another sleepless but remarkable night, called his boss telling him he was not coming in to work any more, that he was going to Louisiana. In three days he knocked at the door of Paul Breden's parents.

They had given him the run of their summer home for two months. "Down on the Gulf, son. Paul loved it there."

Now, on his final morning, he was recounting all of it.

Something took him back to the sneaker, as if Paul was directing him. He heard him say, for the hundredth or more times, "There's so much adventure there, Jadon. Don't miss it."

He picked up the sneaker. It was dry. Had not been in the water in some time, full tide had been mere inches away. Maybe an incoming wave had tossed it higher on the beach. Jadon looked for the mate, for a footprint, for a place from which it might have been tossed. All the beach was pristine for this day, as far as it had advanced.

He put his hand inside the open heel. He felt queasy, someone's sweat, the way sneakers gather up sweat and stink, maintain it. If it had been in the water and was now dry, it might be clean enough. Clumsily he felt the shape of something inside the sneaker, jammed into the toes. The lacing was tied tightly about the object, as if to keep it contained inside the sneaker. Intrigue came upon him. Fishing inside, he felt a tube-like structure, a small round container.

Undoing the lacing with a little difficulty, he pulled the container out. It was a much like that used by druggists to dispense pills, plastic, but there was no prescription label attached.

The little plastic bottle had a tight white cap on it and a note, clearly visible, inside. The note was dry. The printing was somewhat neat and legible.

97

Whoever finds this: My name is Carlton Maxwell. I was visiting in Chapacteau. I was looking for a canoe that got loose and floated off downstream. I saw some men kill a man and carry him on their boat. They caught me and took me too.

I have no large bottle to send a message in, just this medicine container I found in the water. I am alone among these men. I'm afraid I can't be saved. I have seen nobody for days, no boats either. I do not know what date this is.

These men stole something and carried something aboard along with the dead man. They carried me off with them and tied me up and later made me work. They said they'd kill me. I don't remember how many days it's been. Two or three times they locked me below the deck during daylight hours. But one night, when they thought I was sleeping after they were drinking a lot, I got my hold of a small can of paint. If you find this, my fingerprints in paint are on the underside of many surfaces on the boat. The gunnels, the bottom of a door, on the hinge side of hatch cover. I've hidden them there as proof of my abduction. I know they will throw me overboard when they are done with me. They tossed the dead man overboard, when we were far at sea, like he had never even been there.

I have no idea where I am or where they were headed. If I jump off I know I will drown. I would do it if I saw a boat near, but they lock me up below deck when a boat appears.

I know the sneaker will float. The medical bottle carries air. I threw both sneakers overboard. I bet the other one sank.

The gent they killed and threw over the side when we were a couple of days out was Black Martin. They talked about him and something about the Carousel Lounge and another murder they had committed there but he had gotten in the way. His fingerprints are in paint on a note I have hidden below decks under an emergency container.

If anyone finds this, the boat has a number on the side that says LA 9176 WZ but I could tell that some of the figures had been swapped in places because of the background.

If you can find them, please find me. If my friend had not died in Iraq, I bet he would be the one to find me.

That last bit crushed Jadon.

Jadon's complexity was a simple outlook on what he wanted to do in life... but he was yet to find that one view that would lock up his energies. The note he read at least a dozen times climbed down through him and back up out of some cell or recess. If he went to the police with it, they most likely would laugh him out of the station. Of that he was sure. A note in a bottle in a sneaker! How ridiculous! Don't bother us! He was ultimately sure that they would see no reason for the sneaker to be involved in any real situation. It was a huge joke.

But Jadon saw immediately that the small tube might float forever on the sea and not be seen; whereas the sneaker, from its inception, from its first design, was an eye-catcher and most perfectly suited for this final errand. Plus, there was the loss of its mate and it would be useless until the end of time.

He wished that Paulie was standing by. "Hey, old buddy," he said a number of times, "wish that you were here. We had some great conversations, saw some things with the exact same eye. I know you'd believe this," and he held the note aloft again.

A whole series of things hit him, a sequence of events that he might swear, if forced into a confrontation about their inception, had come to him from Paul Breden, late of this world. He saw the police laugh again, not at the note, but at the sneaker. So he made half a dozen copies.

The police, of course, did not laugh him out of the station, but did say it was a far-fetched joke of sorts. "A sneaker?" the sergeant at the desk said. "When's the tap-off for the next game? We'll get back to you, son."

"Can you check to see if this Maxwell guy is missing?"

"Right to it, son. We'll have it checked out. We'll look for him, you can bet on that. That's a promise."

Of course, all that dropped out of context and contention. Nothing made the papers, not a word surfaced about a missing person. No face. No person. No memory. And Jadon Calix was by himself in the matter.

Of course he never saw Maxwell, who never rose up any place in the Gulf. Three months later, Jadon came back to

Louisiana, Paul Breden constantly after him to "find" his Louisiana. And he kept thinking it meant to find Maxwell.

The Bredens, knowing of his plight, allowed him use of their summer home again, and another turn at the beach. He started policing boatyards, the old boat registration number and all its possibilities computerized at first and then locked into his mind. He put an ad in the newspaper about a missing person named Maxwell. There were no replies, not a single one after two more months.

One day, at a lunch counter near a boatyard, he met a girl who was working at a painter's easel. Her black hair, dense as a jungle, hung over her eyes and he wondered how she could be making much of what she was looking at, or studying, he later admitted. She was painting a scene of a boat at a pier and the pier in a motionless harbor. She was a pretty damn good painter and her name was Judi Pless. She had known Paul Breden in grade school. Interest was heightened in both directions when he told her Paul's last words. She liked Jadon immediately thereafter.

The sudden intensities he found in her paintings, the "hold" put on energies that any moment might leap from a hundred sources, captivated him. It was not the colors that did it, or the mix of them by shading and whatnot, but the imprisoning of the collected sense of energy. He found that she had brought some fantastic marine life to a still picture, which would soon go back to work, but for the moments of her study of it, the intensity was in painted surfaces.

Judi was very curious about him, and more so when he explained how he felt about her capture of energy. Her intrigue grew quicker over lunch and coffee.

"Where up north do you come from?" she said, brushing hair out of her eyes, letting him see the sparkle suddenly residing there, the interest coming focal. The shape of his face pleased her, the eye of the artist making measure, finalizing in a way an acceptance.

"From a little town north of Boston about a dozen miles." She liked how he looked at her when he talked, as though his eyes were hungry. "It's called Saugus, but just a few miles away, on the ocean, is a place called Nahant." She also liked his juxtaposition of interest points. "Once, long ago, I saw an exhibition of paintings there by a marine artist. All of them of huge ships and derricks and wharves and gantries and stevedore gear of all kinds, from ports all around the world, Scotland, England, India, like energy at rest in busy harbors. Your work reminds me of his work, but of all of his paintings there was one simple one with a few dories tied up loosely at the ocean's edge, at a place in Portugal, by the mouth of the Aveiro River. Ropes were tied from the dories to branches driven into the sea bottom. It was the difference from the huge gantries and ships that haunted me at first, and then I saw what he had left out of the picture, and what he *wanted* me to see, I was convinced of that. So I wrote a poem about it, about what I saw that wasn't there.

Slowly, without a bit of hesitation, sure of his own words fitting the intent of his message, he recited the poem for her, her eyes steady on him as if making him her new study, her chin beginning to soften in a tell-tale way, lips slightly ajar.

When he finished Judi Pless nodded her understanding, then said, "Now I see what you meant by capturing the energy in my paintings." She, in that short moment, had been captivated herself, could feel it working through her body, making strange demands in its own right, leaving a trail her mind would follow later in the night. "You're the first one ever to say that, how I felt about a stand-still. That's marvelous, how you say that, how you said it. Now tell me what really brings you down here to Louisiana again, whatever it is beyond Paul Breden."

She was expecting something entirely different from this man, a kind of intensity that enveloped him, that was broadcast from him in spite of his most handsome profile. She admitted he had taken her breath away with her first look at him. The depth acclaimed in his eyes was new to her; and she had begun to measure it. All he said in the following moments still came as a total surprise. This stranger, this Jadon Calix, was clearly invasive, had a way of inserting things, of creating interest. She almost said aloud how interesting he was, the words being tasted on her tongue, at her lips. Movement came through her loins, she was positive; it had been a long time for such a breech of faith,

101

swearing there'd be no men so soon coming at her at an angle, designing from the outset.

Jadon Calix read Carlton Maxwell's note to her, his voice steady, his eyes as riveting as anything she had ever seen, seeing what was driving this man.

Then, an angelic light falling on her face, her hair suddenly in place as if set forever, she made him read Carlton Maxwell's note a second time. She kept nodding as if each scene or part of a scene was being set for her eye, for her mind, locking it up, keeping it for added contemplation. "There are things there, in that note, that grab me and then twist me. It's like I am seeing things he did not say, like your Nahant painter friend that made a poet out of you." He thought her to be in that trance-like attitude she called on when she was studying a subject to paint. Jadon could feel her deep resonance, as if she were searching for meaning or resolution. "The police won't help?" she said. "They don't care? How can that be? They should pursue all possibilities. Every damn one."

They talked about other things that interested them, the sea, how it touched in harbors, how harbors touched her, and, lately, him here on the Gulf. They spoke about the Pacific Rim and Pacific Platelets and the California Faultline. It was like a classroom filled with interests. *The Old Man and the Sea*, came and went, along with *South Pacific* and *Moby Dick*. She was stunned when Jadon told her that Michigan had the longest shoreline of any of the original 48 states, where she thought it would be Florida or Maine or California. She did not doubt his knowledge.

Jadon, despite all his other interests, was smitten with her, drawn continually to her good looks, the way her hair would often seem to catch itself in a very special light, as if those shared lights were setting up her pose. And the message in the Aveiro River poem kept popping up in the conversation. She came back to it a number of times as if a new thought had struck a tangent with it. "I think Carlton Maxwell is saying the same kind of things that Peter Rogers said; find the missing boat, find the missing fingerprints. I think he's really saying 'find the missing men who killed that man and dropped him at sea,' and," she paused, brushing her hair back, staring at Jadon as if she was looking through him at another scene, "'find those men that killed me.' I think it's very obvious that he's been murdered. They couldn't and wouldn't keep him around this long, not with the slightest chance of him getting loose. We have to find that boat. It all boils down to that."

"There's a lot of water out there, a lot of boats in ports, and hundreds of miles of shoreline. How do we do it?" Jadon was torn in his attention span; Judi Pless was working all the secret places in his body, all of them, and it began to unnerve him.

He was, at one moment, about to kiss her, thinking how good it would feel, how good she smelled, the way she could look at him as if he could be, would be, a subject for a new painting. And in that one moment of indecision, when he felt at a total loss for all that he felt, Judi Pless leaned over and kissed him right on the lips. "I never do that," she said, "never. I think something might happen here. I'm hoping that it does."

Jadon almost caved in at that kiss. He remembered Paul Breden out on the Iraqi desert, the mortars, the car bombs, and he could smell the scent of death. But this marvelous woman had cut through something a long time ignored with a simple yet not so simple kiss. "I hope so too," he said, feeling his mouth drying up, a choke catching in his throat, a bubble threatening to burst in his chest, his fingers gone itchy. The dawn from an earlier day came back to him in its lavender touch; he could smell the lilac bush his brother had planted some twenty years ago, how a spring evening in the backyard could almost fracture him, and he was almost overwhelmed.

But Judi Pless left that alone for one second more.

She tossed her head nonchalantly, the dark hair bouncing about her face, masking something. "Would you like to come up and see my etchings?" she said, and without waiting for an answer, took his hand and walked off toward her small studio at the head of the marina.

Jadon was amazed at what Judi had accomplished in her painting. The studio, to the walls and shelves, was full of paintings of all sizes, and all bordering in or on the sea. Boats. Shorelines. Rocks with a sea pounding at them. Silent sand under the sun. The paintings leaned on baseboards, lay piled on shelves, were hung indiscriminately on three of the walls. Three harbor scenes at dusk hung on what he presumed to be the bathroom door. When he flipped the paintings over, like others he had turned, he saw the legends. "There's so damn much here. You've recorded all data on the back, just like a newspaper caption, like a journal or a diary of every painting. Your whole life is here. You could spin your whole life right out of these paintings, flip them and make a movie. Still life to action, let the energy loose again. God, you're ingenious. You're thorough. You're so beautiful at what you do. How old were you when you started painting?"

He had come so close to her his breath was held in awed silence.

"My father was painting when I was a kid, he always painted. He'd paint a scene and sometimes throw it away the next day. He was not very good at it, but he was happy mixing and slopping and making crude angles in scenes. My mother yapped at him a lot. Painting was, I think, a way to get away from her. Out in the garage he'd paint anything, whether he liked the scene or not. I wanted to tell him for years, to suggest things, changes, other ways, techniques I could see very early on but I couldn't do it. I wanted to talk about color mix and shading and linear stuff at an angle, but I couldn't bring myself to do it."

Her confession went the whole route, pouring out of her, her face lit up from a mysterious halo. "When he was dying from throat cancer, he said, 'You always knew, didn't you? I knew it and you never said a word and I loved you for that. Now take every damn one of my paintings and burn them before your mother thinks she can sell them. I don't want them seen by anybody. I don't ever want them connected to you in any way. I know that you knew, even when you were a kid. You were special then. You are special now. You will become very special. Find your place in all of this and then kick the hell out of it. Promise me that, that you'll kick the hell out of it all.' He died holding my hand."

In love! In love! Jadon knew he was in love with this painter with the dark lashes and the dark hair and the light leaping in her eyes. He knew incandescence, the mysterious halo burning about them. He knew what ambience was, how it was meant to

104

be. Was this Paul Breden's Louisiana? Was this part or all of what Paul knew he'd find in his Louisiana? He kissed her without another second's hesitation and she trembled and nestled in his arms and then, abruptly, tried to say something, but he was holding her the same way he had held Paul at his dying breath. The end or the beginning was on top of him, around him. The heat of the desert had been overpowering, burning right down through his throat, into his guts all at turmoil. He could taste the acid of gunfire, of shrapnel almost in flight, the dust ready to bury both Paul and him. But in his arms she was struggling, whispering, "The numbers. The numbers. I remember the numbers!"

He could not let go of her. He wanted to hold the moment forever. But she kept saying, kept scratching at reality, "The numbers! The numbers!" Finally, she broke loose, then came back into his arms and kissed him again. It was a long and passionate kiss and then she struggled anew. "I know those numbers, those letters," and with that broke free of him again and started tossing paintings aside after looking at them. "Help me, Jadon, help me!" she screamed. "I remember those numbers! I remember the numbers, the boat."

There were hundreds of paintings stored in her small studio. It was as if they were old magazines or newspapers to be discarded, the way the two of them tossed paintings aside, off the walls, off the shelves, from piles against the baseboard. And in a moment of serene triumph, her hair thrown back over her brow, her eyes full of fire and knowledge and final resolution, she held up Carlton Maxwell's boat. The alphas and numbers were there, caught forever on the prow of the hull, even to the distorted shading of the background where the registration numbers had been switched around.

Judi Pless had listed the date, the marina, the slip number, the harbor, the city. The whole scene came leaping back at her; the masts and bowsprits of other boats at the marina, a small sloop out on the bay, a boy standing in a nearby dory while holding a fishing rod, a whole ball of energy at an utter and complete standstill.

Jadon Calix could almost see the painted fingerprints on the underside of the railings that dipped down the length of the boat. "Let them duck this one," he said, as he kissed her again.

Driving on the Sausage Run
(*Une tranche de vie*, inbound)

This morning D'Espirito "Dez" Carmine knew that one of his passengers was in trouble.

Dez shifted gears of the twelve-seat bus as he came out of Revere onto the highway north, his eyes, as ever, studying the dozen passengers on their way to work, determining a snarl, a scowl or grimace, as a straight-out giveaway. Oh, they were splendid facial characters, make-up aficionados, the mostly imperturbable cast for his play-going. Each one of them he knew almost intimately, their habits, likes and dislikes, their temperaments; how they showed impatience or worry. The lip biters were evident and the knee tappers, the finger squeezers and the puckered, silent whistlers. Who slept around, who was prone to wander come of an evening after work, he knew. Evidence of it came from eye flight or hair disarrangement, an early exhaustion showing itself off or a head yet rolling in a kind of rhythm. The morning body electric, he heard a voice say in the back of his head.

Dez, for that matter, had no sense of guilt for his diurnal intrusions. None of the cast of characters would even have guessed that he long earlier had repositioned the rear view mirror so he had a better view of all of them, including MaryGrace Poplucca and Troy Aquanders seated directly behind him in seat No.1 and opposite in seat No. 2 where sat Jose Negrada and Miriam Hosto. The four had been paired off for more than two years, as if their names were stitched on the seats. In his mind he had numbered the seats, behind him, left to right, 1 and 2, then 3 and 4, and finally 5 and 6. The full bench-like seat across the back end of the bus was reserved for coats, parcels, or whatever the day brought for them, coming and going. There were days that the rear seat looked like a flea market, strewn with toss-outs, collectibles, souvenirs of one sort or another, the makings of a special lunch or affair at noon hour or after work. All of them worked in the sausage plant in Peabody, lately moved from Revere, a forty-minute ride north.

This morning one of them was marked. He couldn't see who it was. Not yet. Worse, he had no idea, not an inkling, of what

106

was going on, what had transpired that caused whispers, asides, and accusations hanging in the air. Eavesdroppers, he subsequently believed, have their own bit of rue, the added weight of knowing half way measures, no full story. For brief seconds he was aware of a small sense of guilt about the replacement of the mirror, what had driven him to do it, yet came with that doubt an appreciation of his passengers; he truly liked them. His wards they were for a piece of the day, two pieces, the coming and the going.

Every morning and evening Dez thought he was on Broadway, front and center with the best seat in the house. The passengers were part of the play that Dez sat in on, every day since he had been hired. They had, some of them, glamorous morning faces, or faces marked so heavy with character and chance that life was here visible in his mirror, every damn angle of it. Once, early on the job, he thought of keeping a journal, about his day and the traffic, about his passengers, but that had gone by the boards as quickly as it had come. Now and then he'd reflect on it as laziness, but managed to also push lack of time into the reason column. The scenes were too much for him not to enjoy, to mark, to measure upon, the daily minute gestures in which to find development.

At the very moment Jose's hand was in Miriam's lap, Miriam in her favorite blue jeans, skin-borne and worn ass-tight, splendidly crotched, at the stop waiting for him so marvelously prominent. Jose's hand was a motionless weight exacting certain demands on the pretty brunette, high forehead of pale skin, almost purple lipstick, her eyes closed, her mouth slightly ajar in a silent salute to an inner feeling, a girl who smiled continually when not at work. Dez had seen that development from the day she had first pushed Jose's hand away from her thigh, a distinct and noticeable act whose energy receded each day. And Dez determined it to be the ultimate seduction by seating arrangement. Jose, it proved out, was relentless and Dez figured he knew the night of their copulation, when, in the morning, Miriam leaned forward, looking up the street eagerly as they approached Jose's apartment building. The sight of him brought her flashing into Dez's mirror, the eyes dark and pleasant and reaching, the way only certain people can broadcast, Dez thought, still liking Miriam no matter the submission. Miriam, he also believed, would not really take a second look at him if it weren't for the mirror. At least he knew that part of the argument.

Now, 5 a.m. daylight falling in the windows of the bus, late April, coffee steaming at his left hand, eyes straight out on the road, Dez said, "Hey, Jose, what do you think of them Sox last night?" He said it as much to Miriam as to Jose, and felt her stir in place, the body language coming to him from off-stage a ways, corner of the eye, the far extent of vision. She was in that early beauty stage so evident in young love, that lift of eye and chin, that mouth so resolutely at memory. The morning Red Sox interruption had brought her out of a mild reverie and Dez hoped fervently that she was not the one in trouble. From the first morning he had liked her, smiling widely, innocent in a warm sense, calling him Mr. D'Espirito as she climbed aboard the bus. "My neighbor in the next apartment says your Aunt Lucy is her friend and told her you got this job. My name's Miriam." Her hand, so recently from bed, from touching herself in morning wash or arousal, was hot and comfortable in his hand. A whole lifetime of dreams she carried in her handshake. Dez had taken to her immediately. That face he would remember forever, the perfect beauty of it, the knowing something and not telling all that shone in her eyes, the art of possibility.

With a slight twist of his wrist, and alert to rotary traffic, he avoided a pothole in the road. Consciously seeking approval, he looked up and she alone of the twelve passengers smiled back at him, an honest and warm reply that seemed to say how well he had handled that maneuver. In a particularly severe move her hair had been pinned back and showed off elegantly small ears and a soft glow riding freely on the mounds of her cheeks. Her mouth, Dez thought, was almost pursed, and made her attractive enough to catch his breath. A small prayer crossed his mind, hoping she wasn't the one this day to be called on the carpet, placed on the coals. Life can get so sufferably fucked up, he whispered to himself, knowing his lips broadcast themselves in the mirror.

The irrepressible Jose, still at conquest, left his hand at attention in her lap. Dez wished the bus was an old regular stickshift so he could shift gears, jam the torque of them. He felt like slamming the whole entity into high speed. Her lips in the mirror were red and puffy.

MaryGrace Poplucca and Troy Aquanders sat directly behind Dez, the two of them usually stiff and formal in their loving, giving little notice of what they were at in their lives, except for the whispers each managed through stiff lips, set chins. She was dark as evening allows itself, clean and brittle as china, always on the edge of being discovered. Troy, in most cases, imitated her; he had become what he loved, and Dez had seen that evolution. Once Troy talked up a storm, about anything and everything, his words and arguments rampant on the air, and now he voiced little about the world around him; no politics, no sports, no restaurant reports or gripes. Nada. He whispered his being to MaryGrace, succumbed, Dez thought, pussy-whipped. Turn in your green card, feller, your time is done. Get rid of your license ID 'cause you ain't the same guy in the picture you was. Dez almost giggled looking in the mirror.

Behind them, in #3 and #4 were the butchers, Harry Kashem and Nate Goodbind, and Nellie McCurry and Penny Angulis, wrappers, widows, whiners. Both Harry and Nate, early drawn together by some instinct for survival, had served time for small crimes, penny ante stuff they would say. They gambled at the beginning and end of day, scratched lottery tickets getting on the bus in the morning, got off at least a full block before their across-street apartments to buy more tickets, even in inclement weather. Neither snow nor rain nor gloom at the end of the day kept them from their appointed rounds. Nobody knew when they scratched a winner, and could only tell the next day when all accounting had been accomplished. In this whole world they trusted no one, including each other. Nellie and Penny, on the other hand, let it all hang out about where they stood on matters, and could say it all and easy and nearly in one breath. "Work sucks. Life sucks. This bus sucks. 'D'ja see that asshole yesterday passing out those forms, like he thinks his crap don't smell."

#5 and #6 were mysterious pairs to some extent. Not because they were most distant in the mirror, and therefore exhibited to Dez less clearly who and what they were, but they dressed in dark clothes, wore sun glasses regardless of the

109

weather, set hats atop their heads not in a rakish manner but one that drew little attention. At times Dez thought them to be fading from his view, diminishing, merging with one another. Max Galatin and Drew Montroy were cutters and stuffers and gave to #5 a sense of inertia. Dez believed that if the small bus caught fire they'd be the last two out; not by choice but by a pure lethargy. Neither one, he thought, drew enough oxygen for the whole day.

The last pair, in #6, two packers, energetic, continually moving as if their jobs moved away from the line with them at the end of the day, were a married couple, Dorothy and Henry Pelican. They worked to send their children to school, and with two doctors to their credit and one lawyer, all high on the pay scale and distant from home, they were on their last child who had sworn to be an astronaut. Daily they dreamed him into space, "into the company of the creatures who surely wait out there for us, not wanting to come here where everything is so foul, so messed up, so unjust where life calls out its every demand, forces all issues to completion."

Dez looked them all over in a scanning and optional study and heard again the words he heard on the other side of the garage wall, just the day before. "I don't know how it was done, but one of them on the bus did it. That's how they got it out of here. And we've got to find it before it falls into hands not favoring us."

Jose, intent on his ministrations, did not respond immediately to the Red Sox opener from Dez. Sort of absentmindedly he was roused from where he found himself to say, "If they hit into any more double plays to kill a good inning, Dez, they oughtta let us in for nothing, not that I'd go then anyway for what they get for parking. That's eight or nine games in a row, and all at home, they drop with a tying or winning run in scoring position in late innings. They need a lefty, they need some speed." A voice popped in from the back of the bus: "They need a life! Face it, them guys don't care if they win or lose they got so much cash coming in. They's frigging playboys, ever one of them. Don't waste no time going there or watching them 'cause they squeeze your balls ever time.

Ever time." Harry Kashem was holding up another losing scratch ticket, waving it over his head. "They's no better than this.

110

Losers. Someone getting fat on the little guys like us. Where you think the money goes from the lottery? It's cut up and divied right under the golden dome, bet on it."

"Why do you keep playing, Harry? You won something last year. Was that crooked?" Dorothy Pelican's long angular face was sour this morning, Dez noted, her eyes depressed, her mouth slack. Dez looked immediately to make sure the first aid kit was still strapped to the corner of the dashboard. Jeez, he thought, she sure doesn't look like she'll get another kid all the way through school. Lightening the weight of his foot on the gas pedal, he wondered how he'd handle things when that moment came, for any of them. She was the one who missed the most work, but was also one of the original workers in the plant, a long-time employee. She had the inalienable rights, whatever they were. Yet, when she didn't go to work, no one would sit with her husband, as if the space would be violated or a disease would be loitering in place. To a person they were deathly frightened of germs or bacteria of any sort, and of salmonella in particular. The true scourge.

Well, he argued with himself, they're not the ones gonna get their asses whipped for something besides the education of their kids. Not the Pelicans. They put every last affordable penny in their last son's lap. Damn, it wouldn't be them, he hoped. Again he looked and thought, by bent it'd be Harry or Nate Goodbind. It goes with the territory, he heard himself say as a northbound Greyhound bus roared beside them, the draft almost sucking in the little transportation brother. What goes in the joint comes out of the joint. Dez's hands on the wheel, bouncing a bit in the wake of the big bus, felt relaxed as Miriam smiled in the mirror at him. Dez felt warm all over his body, and he pictured her that very morning stepping from the shower wet and warm and eager. Her eyes looked like Oreo cookies, big goddamn Oreo cookies looking right down to his toes. He swore he could taste her. The Greyhound bus was nearly out of sight. Miriam, he swore again softly to himself, could probably read him right through the damn mirror. Why the hell did he ever move it?

"Don't you hate them smart-ass bastards, Dez, that sneak up on you like they want to kiss you and then dump crap on you?

111

Don't you hate them bastards!"

Harry was pointing to the big Greyhound bus moving rapidly off in the distance, square back end getting smaller, the whoosh of its passing still hanging an echo about them, as if the air had not yet returned to its place.

Dez jammed his foot down on the minibus' accelerator, felt a shift of weight and balance, looked at Miriam looking back at him, reading him again. I'm supposed to do the reading, he uttered behind his lips, and let a dim smile hang in place. The fast-disappearing Greyhound had him thinking that perhaps just behind him, on the road north, bound for work, someone was looking at the ass-end of his little bus passing through, receding, wondering where the day would bring it, and those it carried.

The Unforgotten

58 years!

Harlan counted again: 58 years!

The numbers were bright as they flashed in his head. In all those years he had made every trip to Wiscasset, Maine but one, the time he was in the hospital in McKees Rocks, PA for his coronary by-pass. 58 years to celebrate a death, a heroic death, but a death forever cold, no matter how hard they tried to warm it up. Harlan Yeats, sitting in the middle seat of his van, looked again at the passing landscape and recognized at least a dozen houses along the road, a huge red maple tree yet blocking the whole front of another house, and the same florist still in business; at least his sign said so. Then came the plunge down toward the center of town, the flag flapping at the veterans' memorial at the curve in the road, where all the names were posted, the universal truth waving its hands.

Harlan Yeats, with his grandson Seth at the wheel, had come off the U.S. Route 1, the Blue Star Memorial Highway, about 30 miles back, after a long hard ride of 725 miles from Pennsylvania. Seth moved the Plymouth van gingerly through traffic building up as they neared the center of Wiscasset. How Harlan loved his grandson Seth, a quarterback from the Valley of Quarterbacks. The litany of quarterback's names ran through his mind: Namath, Unitas, Marino, Mitchell, Fleming, the great, the near great, the poor pretenders. Seth, he was sure, would make his mark, though he was only 17. And after all, he had volunteered to make this trip, to drive his grandfather to a lonely celebration in a small town in Maine, where his grandfather might be the last man standing, the last man from the incredible patrol, Bert Scrubbins's Squad, Wiscasset's own Bert Scrubbins!

The man nobody in Wiscasset knew!

A center of tiredness expanded in Harlan's body, made itself known, pulsed at extremities, weighted his senses. The long haul of his years was on him; it clutched at him harsh as a pair of vise grips, tenacious, always speaking their mind. Breakfast had been by-passed trying to save time, and growls cursed their way in his gut like tired or spent grenades. All the imagery around him made mention of the old squad; sights, sounds and smells, the

113

whole lot of them. The late afternoon sun on the vehicle's chrome crept its silver glare heatedly into his eyes as if it came off a rifle sight, had done so for the last 30 or 40 miles. On the near corner a youngster beat at an old washtub with a broken baseball bat; it was not musical but it was sonorous and strangely warlike. And the air, crisp, moving furtively on the unmistakable aroma of fried dough, made the day seem festive when it was not festive. All of that was outside him. And all of it was measurable.

There were, however, the endless paybacks or trade-offs: inside him, at his backside, sat a pain he swore was over fifty years in the making. "Old is as old does," he remembered his father saying, almost 60 years ago. "The pains and bruises you get now, you'll know again after you're fifty years old. Like instant recall, they'll come back with age."

A bit gruff even to himself, Harlan said in the subdued voice he used when driving alone, or now riding as a passenger by family mandate, "Perhaps all of this began back there, the day we met Bert Scrubbins in Basic."

He coughed and hacked a bit and knew a few other pains that fit him like a sweater. Once again, as if in a daily chore, he was locked into the memories. He wondered if any of the others would come, were able to come, or, in all the odds at work against their long devotion, would come no more, would never be seen again. There had been two of them last year, he was pretty sure. Sometimes he was not sure who the other one was. It was as if they were saints or sinners, their not belonging together being an unsaid guarantee, a silent dictate, keeping no contact in the year long parting, but coming on this same March day for fifty-eight years. A promise made is a promise kept.

"Hell," he said to himself in the gruff voice, as he remembered his comrade's name, "Karl Waggoner looked stiff as death itself last year, the way his eyes wore that deep-well look, the way he knew again something we all had known once and had tried to forget, though a promise said we couldn't let that happen... that we were dead men. It was Mung-dung-ni coming at us again, coming through Karl's eyes. The freeze was upon us, our rations gone, cut off from our company, chill deep in our bones. Tocci and Burpee and even *Old Man* Remnitzer had that same

114

look on their last visits up here to Wiscasset, the way some men get tagged with a look or an aura or a feeling they never quite shake. The kind you might wear for your whole life. We weren't cowards, though we had been scared to the bottom of our souls."

Harlan shivered. It was real all over again.

Seth, at the wheel for six solid hours this day, yet still thoughtful, said, "Tell me what happened, Gramp. Tell me again." His eyes were in the rearview mirror, and Harlan could almost recount the times the story had been told in the kitchen at home, in the front room of the house with company afoot, on the porch of an August night, the moon on the treetops, fireflies on the wind whistling on the pond. What it really said was separation.

Harlan sorted himself into small parcels for measurement, self revelation. Always neat, a sworn recycler of waste products, wary of the turn of Earth into some wildly cataclysmic eruption if kept being handled this way, he tossed his day long cigar, unlit for more than an hour, out the window, into the gutter. He marked it as betrayal. Over his shoulder he looked for a police car to start tailing him, shrugged off the idea, thought of Bert again, coming down the hill in the valley at Mung-dung-ni, the banshee wail leaping from his lungs, the Browning automatic pumping away at his hip the way Lee Marvin or the gymnast Burt Lancaster might have handled it. The twelve men of the patrol surrounded, stripped of weapons, ready to face their Maker, the Chinese itching in their way to get their boots off, take some of their clothes, the wind fierce, the mix of snow and sand and gravel grit from empty bunkers whirling in their faces. The vision never left him, the war silent around them until Bert started yelling like he was a crazy man, the man that nobody in Wiscasset knew.

Harlan continued with his tale. "From the beginning there had been *this thing* with Bert Scrubbins: nothing ever surprised him, or fazed him. He loved the Earth and about all that was on it; the deep woods, the trout streams born of dreams, the place 'where a man hears the ready voice of God in the underbrush and in the white water.' He really said that, like he was reading from the lectern or the podium. From the outset we had noticed all that, but decided that Bert was not placid or immoveable. It was more like he was ready for whatever came along, no matter what direction it came from, no matter what form it took. Once he said to us, 'Back home, in the woods, it can go bad in a flash, in a blind second. I been there, believe me. Best be wary and be ready for whatever comes. You don't stand up to it, it runs you over in a damn hurry.' And he had made the following pronouncement as if a sermon was being finished: 'I ain't one for getting run over.' It was almost like he had bowed to that belief, had made an oath."

"Nothing else really stood out about him, not that man. He was slim. Not very muscular at all. Could only breathe through one nostril, which gave a twang to his voice you'd recognize in a noisy crowd, or a noisy bar. Said his nose had been busted up by a bear. You'd also notice his eyes if you were around him a lot, especially if anything was going on. And when nothing was going on, too, when all seemed quiet. You knew he was hearing things he paid attention to, as though something was hanging on the next edge, something primal, mythic."

Seth's eyes found his eyes wandering a bit. "Like what, Gramp? Something spiritual? Other worldly?"

Harlan smiled easily. This quarterback of his was a reader. That you knew as soon as he opened his mouth.

"Once, on night maneuvers, the peepers still, the frogs too, he heard on the air a fox pup crying like he was caught in a trap. He went off to look and when he brought the fox back to the company area, the captain wanted to court martial him. He made such noise to that end. Bert dropped the fox, which quickly scampered through the captain's legs and raced into the mess tent. The subsequent mess in the mess tent quelled any processing of paper reports. A truce had somehow been established between Bert and the captain."

"The old Browning automatic rifle above Mung-dung-ni," Harlan recalled and said with a sudden tremor, "began its chattering screams just after the banshee cries swept through the Chinese ranks. The Chinese spun at the sound, then froze in place. To a man the dozen of us on the patrol, near prostrate, ducked deeper in the trench as the spray from Bert's Browning slammed into cotton padding, into soft bodies, into the 20 or 25 men who had crept upon us huddled in a bunker and a trench at the bunker entrance. All of us couldn't get inside the bunker, and we had changed places during the night several times, getting momentary warmth once inside. Everybody forgot who had fallen asleep at the switch. Nobody ever said whose turn it had been when we were suddenly under rifle points, stuck at the point of bayonets. Oh, we had heard all the stories, of finding GIs with their boots gone or their parkas or their gloves, the Chinese being re-outfitted. We knew we were going to get at least partially stripped. We also knew that a long cold walk was in front of us. That's the kind of contemplation makes a man shiver to the bone. And we shivered."

He looked back over his shoulder again. No police car in sight.

"It was Bert Scrubbins who prevented that long walk into what was going to be, for sure, at least four years of captivity. It was Bert Scrubbins who had gone off in the night to relieve his bowels. An unbelievable ache, he said, was tearing up his insides. Later, minutes later it seemed, after the threat, after the capture, after the thought of being near-stripped in the freezing cold, after the laying down of arms with rifles pointed right in our faces, it was Bert Scrubbins who came screaming up the other side with the Browning at his hip, the screams terrifying, ungodly to say the least, and the bullets shearing through the night, the surprise hanging out on the air like a million to one shot coming home the winner. He ran right at the clustered Chinese, did Bert Scrubbins, ran at them like a fullback coming right up to the line of scrimmage, all bone, all beating, all power, all a frightening, awesome sight."

Harlan's voice had a new pitch to it, a matching tone, as if it were in concert with his memories, had risen to the occasion. "The noise was a match for the vision of Bert. The Chinese tried to scatter. Some, in close quarters, dropped their rifles. Some tripped over one another. Many of them fell with the pain of bullets not really felt yet, as if waiting for morning to make its call. One of them fired his weapon at Bert. It was the last shot the man ever fired. The last shot the boy ever fired, for that's what he was, just a boy, maybe fourteen. His face was smashed by more than one bullet as Bert aimed a burst back at him, and then sprayed the rest of the Chinese with another burst. Then Bert fell to his knees, that boy's single round lodged in his chest. He

117

managed to send one more spray into the pile of Chinese. Their moans went out on the air. Their lives over, at an end. The last moan was yet a cry of surprise. And that was completed in a moment. Tanbury, as timid usually as a baby, leaped for a weapon, jabbed a bayonet into the last sense of movement."

"On his knees, never-surprised Bert Scrubbins made the only docile sound any of us had ever heard from him. 'Don't forget me.' In the middle of death, in the middle of war, he simply said, 'Don't forget me. I don't want to be forgotten. Nobody at home knows me. Nobody in the whole town ever knew me. I spent my whole life in the woods.' He coughed. He gagged, and spit out the last words he ever said, 'So, please, don't forget me.' He died before any of us could treat him, or stop the blood. He died there on the side of a mountain 10,000 miles from home. He died in front of all of us he had saved."

Seth tried for a change of pace. "Who was here last year with you, Gramp, when Grandma came?"

It didn't work. "I think there were only a two of us. Me and Waggoner. Tocci and Burpee and Remnitzer might have passed on the year before, I'm pretty sure. Somebody called one day, I can't remember when, maybe the summer before, and said some of them were gone. Now, I don't know what to expect. Who to expect, if anybody at all. Waggoner didn't look too good last year, but he never has looked any too good, even way back. Skinny as a rail, he was, and no hair on his head." The pause, the silence from the middle seat of the van, was as big as a block of ice. It filled the van, expanded, and touched Seth at the back of the neck. His grandfather, he assessed, could talk without speaking.

Seth, in turn, did not want to turn around. Nor did he look in the rear view mirror, but said, in his most confident voice, the way he called plays in the huddle, "Well, my gramp will be the last man standing and Bert Scrubbins probably knew that all along."

The van had started downhill into the center of town. Harlan Yeats, in a series of sudden sounds, heard at the back of his head Bert Scrubbins's banshee screams again. Then he heard the Browning sounding like a jet engine. Then, not quite musical, but in a demanding tone, he heard the young boy beating the old metal

118

tub with the broken baseball bat. The boy was all of 50 yards behind them. But the sound was louder now than before, beating like a martial tattoo.

Then, as quickly as Bert Scrubbins had come from out of the Korean night darkness more than half a century ago, Wiscasset, the little river town in Maine, the quiet town, the town that didn't know Bert Scrubbins, came alive.

Wholly alive!

It was miraculous and noisy and bump and run! People poured out of driveways, from between buildings, out of alleys and the two side roads, out of parked cars and vans and trucks all along the main road. Boys and girls and men and ladies, like the total population. They waved their hats and their hands. Gayety filled the air. Faces wore grins and huge smiles. Lots of kids were on bikes. A band broke into music from a hidden place, off behind some building. A trumpet sounded above all of it. Then another. Clarion calls. Ahead of Harlan and his grandson, three or four peddlers pushed their little four-wheeled carriages into sight; balloons fluttered, little flags waved in a slight breeze, Old Glory jacking out in a dozen sizes. The band music was also louder, and its drums began a distinct rolling sound, the way *Assembly* might sound. Harlan Yeats wanted to salute someone. Anyone. The blood pounded in his veins.

Seth Yeats, Quarterback from the Valley of Quarterbacks all the way back in the state of Pennsylvania, thoughtful letter writer, thoroughly pleased that his letter to one reporter in Wiscasset some months earlier had found a true vein, smiled inwardly. When he looked into the rear view mirror, the old man who told stories on the porch in the summer twilight, who shared time with fireflies, peepers, and the frogs in the nearby swamp, who had never forgotten his comrade, was looking him straight in the eye.

Acknowledgment, unsaid, was direct as an arrow.

Harlan Yeats was no longer the only man, the last man, who would remember Bert Scrubbins. The dying plea of a hero would not rest upon the shoulders of an old man. A sign began to flutter on the front of a building down the street. Harlan Yeats could just about make out Bert Scrubbins's name written across a large flapping map of Wiscasset, Maine.

Part of the newspaper story that day, said, in great black headlines, "He was one of yours. Now he's one of ours!"

The Sentencing of Madrigal Orpic

It all came back to him in a maddening rush, the face in the window and the lady with the frail arms. At the moment his body felt hollow, his head light.

Bartholomew Bagnalupus pushed a leafy limb aside and looked up at the window in the minister's house. My God, the face was there at the highest window as if it had never gone away. It was gaunt and pale and tortured in a sense. Somehow, though, it was pulling at him in a weird sort of way, magnetic.

The eyes of that face, he swore, were hollow, set so far back Hell could have sat there more than a visitor. If he had run across the street to tell his father the first time he had seen the face, there would have been an instant knock at the side of his head. In the pantry or the kitchen, at a distance, his mother at pie or pasta would have *tushed* him into silence. Her hands would have said such apparitions do not count, have no place in daily converse, are less than legitimate. Her fingers would have waved him off, the flour like a mist of snow falling from the work of those hands, from the gestures.

Hell, ghostly tales brought with them only mock consideration, if any consideration at all.

"But I saw him, Momma. With big eyes and a scary look in them." Her *tush, child* returned to him this night as clear as a night cry of his daughter might come to him. And he saw again the back of his mother's wrist wiping her brow. He could remember the flour mixing with her sweat, the back of her wrist as if checking her temperature.

"Such a kid, he is, poppa. Such a kid!" her head turned, her voice moving across her shoulders to another room; and he could remember the clarity of such far off occasions.

But for now the face was real again. It had always been for him as real as the window, round, high in the peak of the minister's house, looking like a porthole on the side of a tall ship. He could not count the nights growing up he had slipped into the brush, parted the leaves, looked up at that face. His heart would be beating; and it was like his face was making noises of its own.

121

And always that face was looking back at him, as if the two of them were night's companions, night's strange company in silent acknowledgment. Once he had thought they belonged together; that one could not be without the other. Never was any name known or any other engagement articulated. It was not Minister Orpic's face. It was not the face of his wife Madrigal. It was not the face belonging to any person he had ever seen around the minister's house.

Apparently there was nobody else, nobody to put that face on.

Now, twenty-five years had gone by the boards for Bart. His own father was gone and his mother sat sullenly in a nursing home, counting his visits. A late Masters degree had come to hand, a family had been started, and a full life was just around the corner for him. Yet, bidden on this night, he had come silently and darkly once again to the shrub line near the minister's house, seeking that face. The unsaid articles of a compulsion had impelled him, their strange magnetic forces at work.

As if old October had its way.

Shadows thick as malts surrounded him. The remaining leaves on bush and tree, starlit and burnished, were crisp yet light with moisture. He could smell the acute but passing sweetness of them. Now he knew the slicing distinction of maple leaves and stain-bearing oak leaves, how the mahogany of them traced a pattern in his eyes. Dew, like a late sap, made the sod slippery. The sole distant star was rebroadcast from the filmy grass at last gone brown. The star was a blip on a radar screen. Behind him, at the corners of the old barn and in the late leaves themselves, the breeze talked out to him. The darkness was cool at his feet, carried a bit of dread from his childhood. Cool October wore its touch of midnight confusion.

And the lady of the house, Madrigal Orpic, was no longer a ready tune at the back of his head. There were no quick notes, nothing near the rhymes and ditties that once were quick to tongue. She was now at her worldly and worthy rest, buried just one week earlier.

God, if Melanie knew he was out here after midnight, she'd look at him in that odd way she could ask a question, like,

122

'Are you insane?' the one arm on her hip bent like the question mark, her eyes in other mute declarations.

Or if the police saw him there would be hell to pay.

Life, he suddenly realized, had rushed him with all its energy this quarter century.

But the face had haunted him since his childhood.

It did so every time he thought of the house across the street from his own house. Every time he woke from a deep sleep all the intervening years the house had been present. A child's midnight cry could do it. Or some contrived timepiece setting him awake. An edge of sadness or discouragement or plain tiredness could do it. It happened every time he thought of the face in the upper window or had seen Reverend Chambers Orpic or his thin, worn-out wife Madrigal Orpic hanging clothes on a line from the second floor porch. The clothesline ran out to a tree in the same shadows and secret darkness he now hid in.

Bart quickly remembered a number of other assessments he had made watching her hanging clothes: *She looks like her arms will snap off hanging up a pair of dungarees or a jacket heavy with water. How does a woman so thin and so weak-looking manage to get anything done at all? Will she not break? Why has she not broken? And with such a music to her name?* The old pictures came back to him, reruns of his peek-a-boo life. One of the constant images was Madrigal Orpic at the clothesline sitting down to rest after hanging the slightest and lightest of wet haberdashery or lingerie, socks, underpants, undershirts. Even the span of a half dozen white handkerchiefs, easier in the breeze than in her hands, made her sit. Often he thought that her life could be capitulated in brief seconds, her body so brief, and there'd be little left for ashes.

Once, he recalled, he had designated her as a survivor, and for nothing other than her endless work at the clothesline, as slow and as dismal as it appeared, as weak. He'd recall the heavy sense of wet clothes as they hung almost listless even in a breeze, and see the thin arms that had set them in place. Somehow he had known that those thin bones would work until her last breath.

Chance, this night he reasoned, had brought him again under cover of darkness. Chance and the flannel-mouth outpouring

123

of Richie Dunbar who worked, as he had since his junior year in high school, for Knobby Calum the plumber. Richie talked like he worked, slow, steady, without knowing what halt was. That was why Knobby Calum kept him on the payroll for so long. And everyone knew Richie to be the neighborhood blabbermouth bar none.

"Take those Orpics up at the parish house," Richie said one night at Rico's Blue Moon Café, three old classmates happening to fall against each other one rainy end of the day, "now that was an odd pair for having God on your side, if I do say so myself." He had added, "Church never bearing much weight for me, you mind. Her gone and now they tell me the old minister's got himself real sick. He's in Time's hands now from what I hear."

Richie could put away the Guinness as if he had come from Galway or Kinsale or Elphin or even little old Ballyspittle itself. "One time the old parson had me put in a goddamn toilet in a closet in the goddamn attic, three floors up. Weird set-up if I do say so. Had to run a service line and a waste line down through those three damn floors, took me two-three days to get it done. Then I suspect they had to get a carpenter to finish off what I had knocked out of place. Took a few liberties, I did, knocking some of those old walls asunder." He swigged again. "Yes sir, some days labor's not the worst of occupations, no bout adoubt it."

"Was there an apartment up there, on the third floor, in the attic?" Bart had leaned over at his flannel-mouthed pal of long years still working his Guinness. "How many rooms? Was the place furnished?" He could see the face in the window again, never knowing the age of the face, never having seen the body that belonged to the face.

"I did think that kinda odd," Richie said, nodding at the barkeep for another round. "Not in the room I worked, though there was a door into another room, but it had a big old lock on it. Knobby'd have my ass if I ever went prowling through a customer's house without due cause. And I had no reason to look in that room except for my own curiosity."

All the stuff Richie had said came back to Bart standing in the darkness. Obviously someone was living up there on the third floor. Someone never outside the house. Someone never let outside the house. Someone ashamed of or who would be a point of curiosity. Bart could not imagine what that person could be like. But he had seen him at the window twenty-five years earlier.

He looked again this night. The single star froze itself in a blade of damp brown grass. He saw it on a leaf moving near his eyes.

Then, as if he had beckoned that unknown person, he saw the face at the window. Bart was afraid to breathe. He was afraid to give his place away. But the face was looking right at him.

Bart, in the clutch of minor darkness, lifted a hand, in a questioning salute. He felt foolish, but drawn by time, and his innate curiosity.

A hand waved back.

It froze him in the October crispness.

He hurried home, unsure of what he had seen, of what he knew. He moved cautiously out of the kitchen and into the bedroom. Melanie only half shrugged as he slipped into bed beside her. At length he went to sleep after seeing the star on a leaf, the face in the window.

Melanie was pushing him awake. "Bart! Bart!" she yelled. "There's a fire across the street. The minister's house is on fire."

The face came at him and Madrigal Orpic's thin arms, the Cracker Jax arms, came at him. His breath was short. A vision came and went. The smell of smoke was ripe and alive. He leaped out of bed and put on a pair of pants and shoes. His jacket was in the kitchen, on the back of a chair. He grabbed it and rushed outside.

Fire engines were there. The flames were licking at the backside of the house. The minister, Reverend Chambers Orpic, was sitting on the running board of a fire engine. He was rubbing the back of his head, looking like Death itself, yellow, comical or caricatured at once. His eyes leaped with the redness of the fire. His cheeks were sucked in, his breath held deep. Bart heard him say, "I don't know what happened. It just went boom! Boom!" He waved his hands around. "Boom it went! Boom, that's all." It was like he was giving a sermon about the final day, the end of everything.

Fire and brimstone and hell all at once.

And *retribution*. The word popped into Bart's mind. He didn't hear it; he felt it.

The chief was standing beside Reverend Orpic. "At least we got *you* out okay, Reverend. That's the important part. Now there's nothing more to do but save what we can of the house." He patted the reverend on the shoulder and walked away, his boots rubbing, making noises, the flames calling him.

Bart waited for Reverend Orpic to say something. The reverend only looked at the fiery house, and then he looked up at the high window and down at his hands. He did not say anything to the chief walking away from him, back to the fire. He did not say anything to Bart standing near him, and Bart must have thought he was looking down into his soul. Bart wondered about the music lady, Madrigal Orpic, the lady of the thin arms, the twigs of arms, the slivers of arms, who had evoked lifelong energy for an unknown cause, for a cause too difficult for the reverend to mention, and surely to maintain.

Bart hustled after the fire chief, calling his name, waving at him.

Caitlin, Tollgate Collector

The sun, angling into her eyes, had come up "like thunder out of China 'crost the bay," and even as Caitlin Bordeaux made music of the poet's words, she couldn't remember his name. Nothing was right in the scene though the day had begun in promise. Nick had just gone through mere minutes earlier, the load piled high on his flatbed rig. Most of the night the truck had been parked in front of her house, the neighbors probably talking again. She didn't care, his mouth still alive on her.

Now here's this turkey of a traveler playing music so loud it was damned oppressive. A '98 Nissan Maxima, gray, four-door; she had identified every car for a whole year, and hadn't dropped a bill or a coin in months. Why would some idiot heathen play music as if he were leading a marching band, and obnoxious music to begin with? Something in the day was going to bother her, she just knew it. Why wasn't the loud music ever something she loved, some Puccini, something with body to it? Or a decent dream song? In the back seat of the Maxima she saw the piled-up blanket moving with slight jerks, some living thing in motion. A thousand and one sights she'd seen in her two years here catching coin and currency; people in the back seat swapping favors, or so still they looked dead, once a huge snake sunning at a rear window. Surprises were never too far away. Obviously this was another one. She wouldn't even hazard a guess.

The monoxide fumes swirled through the door and her own cubicle exhaust system sucked them up, but the stream passed around her, touched her. Every time out it made her think of Bill Gennaro's garage back home in Indiana. They'd lived upstairs for ten years and oil and gas fumes and the smell of car rot she thought were environmental, were part of the universe.

It came again with the Maxima, odd for a car only four years old. Would the fumes cling at her skin, age her quicker than another job? In one glance she looked at the mirror propped up in place on each shift she came to work. Some of the collectors kidded her about it. Only Chauncy in the next booth had refrained from ragging on her. Every day thousands of people handed her money and looked at her, eyes at times so leveled and so

127

degrading she'd want to smack them. Thirty-four she was and holding on for the ride. So far there was but the hint of wrinkles, and a thin line curving down beside her nose and getting lost at the corner of her mouth. The teeth of her smile were attractive, she believed, which made her smile reassuringly, an inner dictate making visible its demands. Blue eyes, hiding a bit of pain as always, might give her away if she let them. Nick said she was goddamn beautiful, but how could she count on that; didn't he smell of oil and gasoline and the fumes that 18-wheelers seemed to lug in their wakes forever, invisible tails of huge road comets. She was resigned that it came from having a trucker as a lover.

It was a ten dollar bill the man in the '98 Maxima had handed her, a good looking guy, maybe fifty, gray hair, but eyes out of a far grandstand, deep, labored, bedeviled. She hunted for more of the poet's words, but the music could have killed her. A diamond on one of driver's fingers, she thought, could pay off the mortgage. She made a face at the music, but he didn't make a move to turn it down. Then her heart leaped! Out of the corner of her eye she saw the high-crowned blanket move in the back seat. It fell partly away from what it was draped on and she saw a little blonde girl poking a straw through the bars of a small cage even as she handed the man his change.

Her heart leaped into her throat. She thought of her daughter Mercy still in bed at home and her own mother sleeping in the next room.

The man looked into her eyes even as he stepped on the gas pedal. The Maxima jumped out northward on the turnpike. The panic was on her, in the bloodstream, her heart jamming her throat. Nick was up the road ahead of the Maxima, the next exit about twelve miles away. Nick, with the lovely mouth, with the great hands, was the only hope. The only hope! Caitlin Bordeaux made her move. Screaming for Chauncy Dewitt in the next booth, she scared hell out of a man and woman in a '95 Chevy. She grabbed her cell phone and dialed Nick's number, praying he had his phone on. She held up one finger as Chauncy ran to her booth and she stepped outside. Cars plugged her lane. The fumes were rampant. She held her hand up for Chauncy to listen.

Nick answered.

"Listen, Nick. Life or death. If you want to see me again, listen." The demand was in her voice, in its ascension, that breathless lift. She tried to shake the scream out of it. "Behind you, maybe three or four minutes, a gray '98 Maxima, man at the wheel. He's got a little girl in a cage under a blanket in his back seat and he's playing music loud enough to drown out her cries." He started to say something but she wouldn't let him and Chauncy Dewitt ran to get his own cell phone. Traffic had slowed. Now three gates were stopped tight. "If he gets to the next exit that little girl could be lost forever." She had to tell a lie. "I called home. There's no answer. It could be Mercy. I don't know." She hoped it was a lie. Oh, God in heaven wouldn't punish her for such a little lie.

Nick's voice boomed back. "What the hell can I do, Caity? I can't stop him. What did you call me for? What the hell can I do?" Nick could choke every time he thought of her. His breath could hide in his gut waiting to blow him up, he thought her so lovely, how her hips would mound, how her mound would hip him. Driving the long days on the road he would play the little games of memory, the recall of taste and wonder, the softest touch coming in a moment of such clarity he could spend hours thinking about it, recreating it, the road spinning out ahead of him apparently in absolute control. Now it was done for sure. The screaming in his ear, making new demands.

"Goddammit, Nick, stop the truck. Block traffic. Don't be afraid of a goddamn ticket." Her voice was ascending. "The Staties aren't going to bite you. Stop the damn traffic! Make a roadblock! It's a little girl, Nick. I swear to god you'll never see me again if he gets away with her. It's only twelve miles to Exit Five."

Chauncy was on his phone and waving at her, pointing back down the road and up the road and then overhead. It was as if he were on television and explaining to an audience what was going on. He rushed over to her booth. "Caity, you sure?" His hand was over the phone and his eyes were wide but he was a new grandfather and a former Marine, a rock-solid man. Balding and rugged and smiling a lot, he never ribbed her about looks, never asked embarrassing questions. He'd come out of the fire-flung jungles of Viet Nam where he'd made life and death decisions by the hundreds, sometimes every day. Kicking in was the old adrenaline on the loose, the "you are it" pin tagged on his chest. The M-16 seemed to be frozen in his hands again. The plea in her eyes came universal, the mother's plea, and the knowledge of thousands of years of motherhood. He bet on her. "I saw him and the kid, Lieutenant. Is that you, Bubba? Yes, I saw him myself. '98 Maxima, gray four-door, music playing loud as hell like he was drowning out her cries. Son of a bitch, I get him I'll kill that bastard!"

It had been perhaps seven minutes since Nick had left, Caitlin thought. Twelve miles to the next exit. If he did 70-80 the Maxima could be there in minutes, the girl gone forever. It was up to Nick. She wondered what kind of a father he'd make. Now he had the chance to show her.

In the Diamond-T, the flatbed behind him piled with new but empty pallets, Nick Pridon saw the sign saying Exit Five was a half-mile away. Never had he met anybody like Caity in his twelve years on the road. Whenever he got to her place it was like coming home. That had to be important. If he went by the exit, let the guy and the kid get away from him, she'd know somehow. That truth snapped through him like a whip. The shift knob fit into his hand firm as her breast. The marvel of Caitlin Bordeaux came over him once more. His feet began to dance on the pedals, the gears taking on a new hum, the light load shifting slightly and Nick Pridon pointed into the floor to a trucker he was about to pass. He could have been saying anything but was obviously in need of some help. The brake pedal banged against his foot, the load shifted with a slight creaking, easily, like a snake in the grass, and the Diamond-T began a hitching slow-down on the turnpike.

The newly cut grass at the exit popped up just ahead on his right and the overpass beyond it where Exit 5 raced off to the west. Four American flags snapped in the morning air above the overpass chain link fence. The Kenworth rig beside him, one that Nick had seen before with a State of Maine map on the driver's door, ground slowly to a halt with him. Behind them came the screech of brakes, harsh screams coming off the pavement.

But there were no impact sounds. Traffic stopped. Nick

stepped down from his cab and looked behind him, back down the road toward the toll plaza almost twelve miles behind him. The traffic all along the pike was coming to a standstill. On a crown of the road, over a quick rise, vehicles coming to a crawl looked like dominoes edging into line.

A man leaped out of his car immediately behind Nick's rig. "It's on the radio. Some son of a bitch has a kid in a cage in his car. Between here and the last toll plaza unless he got past us and took this exit. The guy on the radio says the police are sending out a helicopter and they're coming down here from Exit 5. Says the guy is playing music loud enough to kill you."

The man looked back over his shoulder. Nick looked. The driver of the immense Kenworth looked. They could hear the music like a hundred boom boxes at work, and down the median strip, speeding on the narrow grass plot, careening, swerving in and out of sudden swales and dips, came the gray Maxima, the heavy music leaping out front of it like the blast of trumpets. Nick looked at his rig. He'd never get it across the median in time. Morning traffic was heavy going in the opposite direction. The man who talked about the radio announcement looked at him. All around them people were out of their cars, some yelling, some saying "kidnap, loud music," some complaining and swearing. The man behind Nick leaped into his car and pulled it broadside across the median just as the Maxima came up out of another deep swale and stalled on a crest of ground.

The man in the gray Maxima leaped out of his car and heard sirens in the distance, their wail as harsh and cutting as screams. When he tried to jump back into the car, half a dozen men pinned him against the side door. Nick pulled open the back door, flipped the blanket off the cage, unlocked the top and picked up the little girl. She screamed in his ears and struggled and he showed her to people gathered around them. A grandmotherly woman reached for the child and held her in her arms. The woman kept shaking her head and clutching the little girl against her bosom.

Chauncy Dewitt, standing in front of ten miles of backed up traffic at the toll plaza, danced across the pavement, waving his arms at Caitlin. He had the phone at his ear. People were all over

131

the road, the radio still blasting out the news alert. Chauncy had called the local radio station.

A gutsy early-morning disk jockey and news broadcaster had jumped the news with an instant headline for the morning travelers. "Here's in-process news breaking for travelers northbound between the Parkman Toll Plaza and Exit Five. A kidnapping is in process right now. A man in a '98 gray Maxima, playing loud music, has a small girl in a cage in the back seat of his car. Don't let him get off the road at Exit 5. It could be your kid he has." He had kept saying the same thing. The police had been called, the wheels had turned.

Caitlin Bordeaux, late that night, heard the engine of the Diamond-T grind to a halt, air escape the connection line, a door slam with a solid thunk, and Nick Pridon's footsteps on the walkway moving toward her. Mercy sat sleeping in her lap as she had for two hours, the night-light on, shadows bouncing around them, a few neighbors' lights throwing off a warm glow.

A Pocketful of Verse

Nothing brings it home like feasting on a poem. (Unknown guitarist on a troopship, outbound, 1951.)

I'm not sure I knew I was setting out on an important journey. The whole battalion had been marching for three days, in the rain, the heat, the Korean miseries. Was something new trying to break into my thinking... journey of journeys? Occasionally a marcher is full of questions, or doubts. In marching there is little to do but gripe to one's self, pray and think away.

Somewhere down the line of my comrades on the march, above the thud of boots, web equipment jostling, grunts and deep breaths in odd unison, came the blast of a whistle. We were two columns of fully armed men, passing each other and going in opposite directions, and for moments stopped in our tracks. Some of us were going back to a reserve area, to rest and hot showers. Some of us, in the luck of the draw, in the other direction. We were beside a company of engineer troops digging roadside gutters to handle the promised seasonal rains coming from the Sea of Japan. Soon, as good as promise, the Sea of Mud would grab at us.

I dropped my gear to take ten and stretch out on the damp ground beside the Main Supply Route, the MSR, on the Korean eastern front, a May day at mid-morning, 1951. The sun rays felt hazy and damp. At the small of my back an ache kept making itself known.

Realization came that silence in the war zone is eerie, and unbelievable. I thought that measurement of a sort was in play, demanding attention. It was, I reflected, like stopping to smell a riot of flowers on a country lane or a manure pile ripening outside an old barn down Maine. Things forever lived and abounded all around me, memories and imagination locked with their noose. The engineers, I noticed to a man, were all black soldiers. The infantry marchers were all white.

I sat up when one of the engineers stood over me looking down, his eyes like sad brown echoes. A smile suddenly striped his face with perfect teeth, affability. The man, I thought, knows how to smile.

133

"Care for a smoke?" The black soldier extended a pack of cigarettes toward me, and then sat down as I drew a single cigarette from his pack.

"Thanks," I said, nodding, looking into the deep brown eyes. "I haven't seen any Luckies in a month of Sundays. What we generally get, at this end of the war, is floor stuff, factory sweepings not worth the bother to collect it commercially, more powder than a grenade sets off."

"Don't mention it," the black soldier said, as if disregarding my claim, "I'm Calvin Boone." Boone extended his hand and allowed a deep, gleaming smile to accompany his outstretched hand. White teeth, square and even, one of them capped in gold the sun found easily, carried contrast to a distance. I thought again, he sure knows how to smile.

"I'm Frank Butcher." The knowledge in my back was teaching me a lesson about what side of my body to lay on, what hip could tolerate the slightest temperature change or an ounce of discomfort, how it could manage sudden movement.

"You guys going back up?" Boone puffed away at his own butt, small exhalations of smoke marking the stilled air.

"Yuh," I countered, though not really up for small talk. "We were in reserve for a few days, but we moved out yesterday. We gotta do it all over again." A pause hung its stripe in the air. "Probably be back up there in a few days and cover the same ground. We did it before so many times, it's like a friggin' game."

Boone looked straight into my eyes. "Do it all over again? The same territory? The same terrain? The same damn hill?"

I spoke from the side of my mouth, like I knew it all. "Yup, we're going back up to take Sugar Loaf II. Blue Item lost it day before yesterday. And that's after we had pitched it in our back pocket. Not that it was a piece of cake by any means." I paused, measured, replied, "It friggin' stinks the way I look at it. Ought to be a realtor here drawing lines, making sides, setting prices, and posting ads. Cover his ass if not ours, if you really want to know." I was sorry I said that, as Boone grimaced, like an outsider let in on a secret.

Boone flipped his cigarette arching through the air. It fizzled in a small pool of water in the main road bed. "Tough that way, ain't it?"

I leaned back and lay on one side, propping my head on one hand. "I don't think we're ready for it, not this outfit. We're not up to full strength for sure. Pulled some of us down the last go around."

"I'd sure like to be going with you," Boone said as he looked back down the road. The company of black soldiers was standing on the side of the road, each soldier holding a long-handled spade. Boone began to rub his palms together.

I looked up at him, one eyebrow arching higher than the other. "Hell, I'd just as soon be back here with you guys digging holes while I was standing up, rather than be up there digging them on my gut." I spit out the side of my mouth. The saliva landed on the edge of his pack. He reached out with one finger and rubbed it into the pack.

Boone rubbed his palms together again, like punctuation of a sort, or annunciation. "It's different with us. They won't let us go up. Not much of a fight lugging a shovel in your hand. I hate to see you guys going by, going back up."

"You guys have a job to do," I offered. "If these roads get mired in, the supply trucks can't get through... no ammo, no good chow, and," I laughed a bit, "no reporters either."

"I've heard all that soap before. It doesn't sound so good when you see a unit go up and they come down a few days later and you know some of them ain't coming back the same way."

I looked at the butt of my own rifle, the plate all scratched, abraded, worn. "Is it so damn important to you to go up there?"

"It sure is when they say you can't join a combat unit because your skin's a different color. Most of us are in transport or engineer units. Makes me feel friggin' useless." He sat down beside me, his hands stretched out behind him, one hand resting on the barrel of my rifle, stretching himself, his manhood.

"Where you from in the states?" I said.

"Jersey." His eyes were like mine when I mentioned home.

"Makes it kind of hard, don't it?"

135

"I never met anything like this at home, not usually. But some of the guys, they don't feel anything different. All of us hope they stop this segregation crap pretty damn quick."

I sat up. "I'd swap places with you any day of the week. In a damn minute. I'm kind of worried about this trip. I almost got wasted on the last trip up there. Never been so scared in my whole life."

"I've been afraid a lot back here, too," Boone said. We get a little incoming mail once in a while. It can't be the same feeling though."

I rolled over on my other side, my legs crossing one another in a deliberate motion.

"Man, when you're getting popped at, it's all the same."

"Difference is you can't hit back with a shovel." Distance and some other reach, some other argument, were buried in his eyes.

I didn't answer. The silence continued on for a long spell, and Boone finally said,

"Where's home?"

"Ellston, Iowa. Population 210. 209 since I left."

"Farm country?"

"Yuh, it is, but my dad runs the general store in town. I was glad to get out of there for a while, but I'd sure love to be back there now." I stared down the road and I pulled on my pointed chin with one hand. Reaching out, I grabbed a handful of earth and let it trickle through my fingers.

Boone lit another cigarette and I looked up at him as the whistle sounded down the line again and the moaning of men arose as they came to their feet.

I said, "What's that you got in your jacket pocket?"

Boone smiled as he said, "An orange. Want it?"

I said, "I'll swap you for it."

"Okay. What you got?"

"A book of poetry. Soft cover. I've been into a lot of it. Probably three or four times through it all the way. Marked it up a bit." I reconsidered. "I marked it up a whole lot, lots of special places in there."

Boone's eyes glowed. "Deal," he said, then smiling, added, "pen or pencil?" His smile was a huge smile. That guy, I swore again, knew how to smile.

I laughed from deep in my gut, reached into my fatigue jacket pocket and drew out the book as Boone handed over the orange. I stuck the orange in the pocket where the book had been, picked up my pack and hoisted it to my back. I felt I was close to some destination.

I slung the rifle over my shoulder and walked off to my destiny, looking back as Boone thumbed open a page, saw a verse I thought he might know because he smiled that true smile again.

I thought he had really gotten to some part of home by looking at my book of poetry. But here, in what might be the middle of a shorter trip than planned, I found a mental marker, a touch of reality. I under-stood I had finally come home.

Red River Shoes

Odd and memorable days often have odd and memorable starts. Sixty three-year old Police Chief Ben Perdy's day was beginning and he didn't know it yet, sun rays still creeping toward his bedroom window, the flash momentary, sleep trying not to let go.

At that precise instant, beside the Passimaquik River at the edge of Nonquit, two town boys came carefully through heavy growth by the river's initial bend near Nonquit Center, their lips shushed, their cameras in hand. Discovery and highlight of the new day came for the boys near the river edge. Sitting on the bank as if a sensual, long legged blonde or redhead had just stepped out of them, was a pair of fiery red high heels. Red, sexy even in their emptiness, but dancing shoes, dating shoes, going-out shoes for sure. The sun caught them in an illuminating shot and quickly bounced away from its own glare.

But there were no tracks, no sign of either long or short journey, no story to go with such abrupt high heel punctuation.

Trouble shoes, each boy thought.

The placid morning rolled around the pair of shoes the way a fog lifts, as though a vagrant artist had placed them there for a vision to collect, paints to speak his mind. Nearby, in the tall and mass-struggling reeds, a remnant April breeze sounded like a comb making its way through old corn stalks. Out of the northeast the rough night wind had stopped its wild gallop, had laid down its head to sleep in the early sun. River waters, at a point of tidal change, sat still as molasses. The whole Atlantic, slicing the far horizon, was still too.

Questions, doubt, mystery all melded in the morning pot.

Ben Perdy rolled out of bed on the button of 5:00 a.m. Without a glass of wine the night before there was no need for an alarm clock. He often wondered if morning birds at high choir did it or some trick his blood performed. Or else a place in the back of his mind that snapped a flag for attention, some other-world retreat he'd been off to. Then, as always, without doubt, Molly Popp's face came at him from that dark distance, sweet Molly, always potential Molly; fifty years a sweetheart and never yet a kiss.

Something electric, deep but not foreboding, moved within him. With an unsure touch he rubbed his stomach searching for an elusive gas pocket that might have roused him.

The youngster Darren was the first up out of the brush, saying to his pal Michael, "Think she drowned, Mike? Think some guy pushed her in, right out of her shoes? We have to tell Ben Perdy. He'll put yellow tape around the whole area, maybe the river itself. And I don't see any pocketbook. There's always a pocketbook hanging around with chicks. They carry their own rubbers. I heard my sister Dollie telling Josie on the phone, 'You got to have your own rubbers 'cause they don't care half the time.' Jeezus, it's like making peanut butter sandwiches to them the way they talk about it!" His head was full of pictures he had seen in a few magazines; red high heels, long bare legs and the other bare mysteries that so often dried his throat, made him feel funny and alone. He wondered if this girl of the shoes had been a redhead, or a blonde, and that hard to tell even then.

Darren Popp and his fourteen-year old pal, classmate and bird buff, Michael Rodden, had come upon the shoes along with the rising and splintering of the sun. Their cameras were ready for the first bird of the day, the first dawn-provoked, colored flight they would get a shot of coming up out of groundcover. Darren carried a Bowie knife, big as his arm, at his belt. A just-in-case investment. Looking about carefully, the boys noted again that there were no tracks near the shoes, not the slightest impression. Not a one. The bank was darkly rich, April soft and muddy and would not dry out for days.

But there were no tracks. The shoes, the going-out red shoes, cried out for tracks, for compliance, for explanation.

Mystified, the boys started back into town, imagination of both boys concocting wild tale upon wild tale. Measurements of some unknown kind were otherwise being contemplated, each one with his own approach, his own angle on the shoes their own riverbank was wearing like a romantic remnant.

"Think we have a murder here?" Michael said, looking back to the Passimaquik River snaking away to the Atlantic, the bends behind him like a huge slow-breathing *S* emptying brackish ponds, upriver flats, other slow streams anteing up their own spring effluence. In the distance, darker than they would be minutes later, the range of hills around Nonquit was also emptying damp April's offerings. The boys knew the hill music the spring waters compounded, for that was a territory of past haunt and old nesting grounds. They could put many memorable birds in the posture of the original sighting, the colors too, and what went on around them, like built-in scrapbooks or photo albums.

Michael pursued his attempt at measurement and his chase at reality. "How do you get a pair of shoes stuck on the banking that way and no tracks around them? In a hundred years you couldn't throw them together like that. Not from the reeds or the brush line. Not even from one of Guy's canoes." He looked back again. "Could have come right from a dance. I wonder what she looked like. Probably had great jugs that got her in trouble, and long legs from you know where. The chief, old Ben Perdy, won't let a soul near that place in a month of Sundays. Like he don't let no one get too near your grandma but never says anything anyways."

All of 5:00 a.m. had touched Ben Perdy with its fingers, letting all his bones know of its arrival. He washed the face of the older man looking back at him from the mirror, blinking his eyes at still having hair on his head and fewer than usual wrinkles at the neckline for a 63-year old man. His eyes, he noted, were as pale green as ever and not loaded with any great weight but his own measurement. That measurement voiced itself: *Getting on, boy*, it whispered.

A good feeling moving in him, calling out to him, he swore he'd reach a song if he could. For a moment he figured it was morning rather than Molly Popp. She had a morning presence he had never told her about, figured he downright wouldn't tell her in a hundred more years, give or take a few. *Little said is little damage done*. Ben Perdy wanted to say *status quo* but it would not come up from where it was hiding.

Day had officially started for him. He pinned on his badge and snugged his belt. For a quick recovery of duties, to reassert a sense of organization (really, he thought, to catch his breath), he gave the day coming a salute full of yesterday's leavings. Art Kornell was in a cell again, for raising hell at Mallory's Pub. Art

140

would need his breakfast and dear friend Molly Popp at her house-diner would have it ready for delivery by 6:30. Yesterday's accident scene just outside town would need another look, if only to ease his mind. Mash Holcumb would still be out of town down to Dunwoody for his grandfather's funeral, and then a day's travel home before he'd come back on relief duty. Amid all that reflection he inhaled his near sixty-three years on and about the river, let it all come back upon him; salt thrush, August fire in the reeds, love-lies-bleeding hanging about the banking near Guy's boathouse, even day-old fish thrown out on the high banks by young fishermen contemptuous of bones. The far mountains behind him, ever feeding the river, would now be catching a bit of the early sun fire. All of it brought him measurements he was often not ready to accept or give away.

Even then, with the sense of organization tossed in the ring, there was nothing unusual silhouetting or daubing the horizon of the new day.

That thought brought him back to Molly; he could see her leaning her goodness against the kitchen counter in the half-house and half-diner, as if all that goodness now and then needed some respite. Her still-lovely and comely being had worn him down long ago. Soft still-red hair would be tied up in a band, with a small portion of her years pushing at the backside of her dress. That part never failed to catch his eye. No calipers could ever lie about or distort the lines of those curves, nor could they abort his wonder about her and the way she might be put together. *I'll never be able to tell her that*, he thought. Though, with him, her trimness counted and extended a mark of reliability. His own weight, controlled by work and practice, pushed lightly and easily against his belt. He felt the vague sense of being comfortable, and also knew the true lie of it.

This morning again, no different than hundreds of others, Molly wholly warmed him, small sparks traversing a mesh of inner wiring he could almost touch. *My own gridline*, he thought. He could easily compound a sense of spark or shock. *Batteries included* came at him with a grin. *Plus*, he thought, *there'll be a sense of cinnamon about her, a pause of kitchen refreshment that could readily move to the bedroom. Or it ought. She'll look over one shoulder when I come into the diner, hair evenly in place, her neck in that graceful curve like it's a tale being told for the thousandth time. She'll smile a kind of radiance, so a whole hearth beckons in the gesture, makes welcome of itself.* And that's when the wire mesh, his own gridline, would generate a gentle kind of ignition south of his belt.

At 5:00 a.m he knew the people of the town that would be awake: there'd be Molly with his and Art Kornell's breakfast in the works, Art Kornell himself, pacing the jail cell in hunger, and Tab Glasser at the gas station on the edge of town keeping his eyes down the road. A few woodsmen would be moving toward the hills and he could recognize some of their trucks by drive shaft whine or tappet noise. *Blues* or *Country* would float down the road. Sometimes there'd be those boys with their cameras out and about, looking for prized migrants heading away from exotic lagoons toward the northern fields and the lean and mean neighborhoods of glaciers. The world, he thought, could drift right by him in a matter of seconds. There were times when he thought it had.

When the phone rang he figured it had to be Molly or Ted.

It was one of the boys, Molly's grandson Darren. "Sheriff, this is Darren. Me and Mikey found a pair of red high heels stuck almost side by side in the muddy bank of the river. And no tracks around them, sheriff. Not a one. It's like they wuz thrown there from the reeds. We thought you ought to know. Ladies' bright red high heels." He added, "The dancing kind," as if he too were at measurement. His voice paused. "Kind of spooky if you ask me."

"'Bout where, Darren?"

"Directly opposite Cosgrove's front door, this side of the big bend. I lined it up, and we took a couple of telescopic shots of the shoes, but didn't go near them. There's still no tracks there."

"I'll check it out after I get breakfast from your grandmother. I got to feed Art."

"He in there again?"

"Grandma gets paid for it, Darren."

"Want us waiting? We got us some interesting flyers here. Won't be wasting our time."

142

"Stay put if you want, Darren. Me, I need breakfast first. I'll be along." As an afterthought of interest he said, "See anything else interesting? Any long-lost pals come along the way?"

Silence was as good as nothing, he figured.

When Ben Perdy told Molly about the red high heels, she allowed a serious look to come across her comely face, as much omen as it was surprise. Her eyes were bright with morning, the same light sitting on her cheeks. She wore a pastel dress and a red apron. Her legs were long as she leaned over the counter. Flour sat a pattern on her apron; another bit was dust on her short sleeve. Ben thought Molly was an aces cook, a sylph if he could have dragged the word out of the past, and that she, like all natural redheads, had those marvelous green eyes bearing all the powers of a spade. He dared think she could have owned him any time she wanted to. And he had long courted on her for sage advice at times. It was part and parcel of her being, and their own small network of two people too long in the fancy of the other, but without direct participation of the ultimate possibilities.

Molly Popp had kept the whisper of her shape all these years, thin and agile, and her hips could still be seen making the measure of the mystical valley. Ben Perdy often marked women by their hips. Ben would fix them in place with their minds. In addition, Molly's hair was always in neat arrangement and she wore no makeup except her continual smile. Once, the two of them gabbing on a Christmas Eve, she told Ben it was the memory of Branner Popp, the only man she had ever known, that coaxed her through some odd days with a smile (as if Branner had never left, he thought). Now that smile had disappeared for a moment with talk about the red high heels. One of her hips dotted his horizon for the barest second, and his flush was slow but crawled toward permanence. On numberless nights she had assailed him and he feared that that dreamy marquee had showed itself again.

"Sounds like trouble to me, Ben. You know how I feel about odd things like that." As if to add punctuation to her statement, or to stress her beliefs, she wagged the coffee pot at him. A breast moved under a large flower on her dress. It too wore the dust of flour.

He nodded and she poured, but he knew she was coming back at him, her head cocked, wonder showing. "It's not just a pair of shoes, Ben. They're not usual around here unless there's a dance or a special time. Red high heels means a fellow's in the mix, being chased or chasing. That's easy enough to see. Red high heels mean finery and a pitch at elegance. Silk underwear, the whole lot." Her face had not even reddened. "I guess I wore them maybe twice in my whole life. Once to Lonnie and Mella-Sue's wedding, and once when Bran and me went up to Wellington to that hotel for the big centennial dance." The way she tilted her head was as much recapture as Ben could assess, but that was plenty enough for him, grandmother or no grandmother.

"I'd look along the river a ways," she said, pouring another mouthful of coffee in his cup. She shivered at her delivery, the vibrations very strong along her spine. It was part of her announcement. Conviction came in the tone of her voice.

Ben Perdy, subsequently in a couple of attempts, looked along the river and found nothing.

Two weeks later, the issue of the red high heels about the last thing on her mind, Molly saw an article in the paper about a missing woman, the wife of a rich industrialist. The woman's husband had flown from the airport at Wellington to the capital. It was a night flight. When he came back the next morning his wife was not at home. After a few days she was declared missing. There was still no trace of her. Molly did not like it, the vibrations and the red shoes locking together in her mind.

Showing him the paper the next morning, she said, "Ben, I got to mention the shoes again. It's only right. I found out some sneaky rumors and stuff about this flyer husband. I went ahead and called a few old pals. He was a ladies man. Rumors about him just won't go away. The plane he flew went from Wellington down to the capital, down at the Atlantic edge. Flew right down the Passimaquik River, out of the hills and right over the marshes. That's a thousand acres of loneliness and pools and lots of brackish marshland south of town. It's a salty delta, enough tidal life to feed forever. That sets me tingling. You ought to know all that, Ben. It's only right. If you don't listen to another woman on this account, one who's not lost yet, not entirely, it'll serve you right."

Molly paused, gave him a new look, and continued. "I won't tell you your job, Ben, but you know how things come at me. I plain think that poor girl was thrown out of that aeroplane. The whole thing stinks to high heaven. I just got this feeling invading me all of a sudden." He thought that if she had the coffee pot in her hands she'd wag it at him.

"Molly, how in hell can I check out a thousand acres?" He swung around on the diner stool, nobody else yet in for breakfast.

Behind the counter those discernible hips of hers were making a statement. He was sure of that when she said, "You ain't saying she ain't worth the extra mile, that poor girl? And him flighty with another one don't know her dues is coming. You saying that, Ben Perdy? Some people stays and pays their dues."

If she wasn't making a promise, she was providing decent room for one. The age-old tingle again became apparent somewhere south of his belt line, grandma or no grandma. He was thinking about prerogatives and intentions, and soon realized they didn't mix with crime or details. A couple of times he and Marsh set out in one of Guy's rental canoes, and plied their way through brackish pools, tide spills and the tidal runs through extensions of the marsh. They found nothing. No lady belonging to the red high heels. No dancing lady no longer dancing.

Molly, at breakfast one day in the diner, not letting go, was at it again. She said, "If I was you, Ben, I'd let someone down the capital have those shoes to check them out. Where they come from, like what store and such. Shoes like that come from city stores. Give them to that guy at the lab you know, and get them out of your mind. Most important, get them out of my mind. I keep thinking about that girl gone missing and her husband flying around doing his thing. That bugs the hell out of me. It surely does. It's time it moved on, if I really got to say it." She turned her back on him, leaned against the stove counter, her charms moving at him, slowly, relentlessly.

He suddenly realized she was charming him, using him. Then, not a wholly new thought either way, he thought he'd like to kiss her anyplace she wanted kissing. It suddenly seemed most appropriate.

It hit Ben Perdy that she knew what she was doing. That she couldn't say any more than he could say; the two of them stuck in neutral, pleasant, hungry, but in a forced neutral gear. He was willing to wager that Branner Popp had known those measurements all the time.

The boys in their pursuit caught up with a few strange birds…and Ben Perdy made more assessments, more broad calculations. The laboratory proved by DNA checking that the shoes belonged to the missing woman. An investigation by capital police ensued. There would be an inquest, even without a body.

All vibrations had been noted, all electrical connections made and understood, all dalliance moved aside on the downside of life, of personal measurement. Ben Perdy walked around the counter one morning shortly thereafter and put his arms around Molly and said, "I wasted enough time, Molly, 'bout half my life. You still got them high heel shoes you wore to the centennial dance?"

The gridline moved, sparked. Molly smiled and said, "You ain't as slow as I thought you were, Ben."

The Dollhouse Victim

Badger Martineau was displeasured. Perhaps it was the cheese in his soup, or another point in making age a paramount factor of life. Whatever worked in him, a bit of a grumble, heartburn, it was fleeting, and went its way, fading like an offshore breeze. His granddaughter Alexa had no part in it, he was sure, for she had considerably brightened each day in coming to the house, to visit, to play, to invest time in the dollhouse finally brought out of the cellar.

It was the dollhouse he had made for her mother when she was but a child of the same four years; some of it made at sea, most of it made in a corner of the cellar a winter or two. When his daughter had outgrown it and moved on to other interests, it languished for years, unheeded, in a dark corner of the cellar. Retrieved for a new generation, he had painted it anew and repaired some old flaws, set new flooring in place. The little house was a scaled down model of the very house he had lived in for more than seventy years, and now it sat in the front room, by a window so neighbors passing by could see it, on a carrousel affair. Soon his granddaughter would have it for keeps. At night a light illuminated its front façade like a billboard advertisement on the Turnpike. *Traveler, take heed. Rest is here.*

From his old and mostly battered but comfortable Morris chair by a side window looking down on the river, eventually the sea, Badger could see all the details of the miniature home; clapboard exterior, double chimneys that gave it a Colonial calling and stamp, two floors with a pitched roof. It was painted white as foam in a good and proper wake. More than once the whiteness had made him think of sails thrusting at their lines, grabbing at a West wind. From the backside he could see the partitions of each room, doors of closets, balusters and rails of banisters, carpeted stairs up from the front hall to the bedrooms overhead. Red brick fireplaces, made of grooved paneling, sat on each wall of each room. The monster chimneys, down through the huge archways in the cellar, had great responsibilities in the house, being the ultimate shoulders. Wide maple floorboards added the grandest touch of character, almost screaming out authenticity in their corn

147

syrup shine, their golden patina.

Yet now, for perhaps the eighth or ninth day in a row, or was it more, a sort of unsettlement had come upon him. He had tried to make the point of remembering when the feeling came. And it came when Alexa was in the house. Always then and never at any other time. At those times he was sure he'd caught a little bit of her mother in her eyes; that look, that dare. But he loved the child so much he threw the thought away like a wild throw to first base, too hot to handle. But it came back to him each time. She'd be at the little house, her blonde hair atop her shoulders, humming to herself, talking to imaginary friends, much as he had done at sea on lonely watches, to a sailor lost at sea long ago or a shipmate who had gone ashore from a most memorable cruise and had never come back, a stretch of pure loneliness. The jabber was a monotone, a humming, a companion for silence, and moved the way a small wave seeks a bay or a sandy beach.

This acknowledged point, this quick rush to notice, only made him more disgruntled with his unsettlement; but for all his years he was a man of details. Alexa, he saw, could be hours at the house, and nothing would come to disturb him. She would dismantle whole rooms of furniture, reset and re-style one room from another's goods, make beds face east and west rather than north and south, swap remnants of rugs, change the character of walls, and thus of rooms. None of it would really bother him.

"Alexa," he'd say, just as a matter of conversation, to let her know he paid attention, to mark a response, "why didn't you like the way that room was laid out? It was neat and proper just the way a trim ship should be." Was there reasoning to her decisions rather than some kind of rote? The Morris chair made sounds beneath him as he leaned forward.

The look would come his way, her mother's look, the woman in charge. "Oh, Grampa, my best friend Joe didn't like it. He said he was tired of it. He's such a good boy. I thought I'd let him have his way. You know, like you do me." The smile floated to him like a lifeline; lost at sea and saved. "Would you want it any other way?" There was the woman again. The voice could bend him, the inflection, the woman coming out of the child. "You could pay me like a housekeeper, like Mrs. Rainette pays old Mrs.

148

Cluskey down the street from our house, like a dime a day. Dad says it's really peanuts, just pennies, he says."

"You are a most marvelous and engaging child, Alexa, much like your mother was at the same age." The strange delights she created ran with the sudden ill feelings he had, as if neutralizing his small despairs.

It was a week later, his mind clear as a bold sky, all his rote now parceled into proper niches, that he keyed onto the one missing ingredient; no matter what article of furniture she touched, little happened to him. But when she picked up the miniature rocking chair he himself had made, modeled after his own grandfather's chair, set it into the exact same position every time in what had been his grandfather's room for years, at the same window, at the same view down the river, the clutching came over him. Displeasure came at once, a kind of despair moving on him, and though he knew it was not directed by this engaging and delightful child, it was she nevertheless who put it into motion.

The contradiction leaped upon him. The connection was absurd, yet it was there. Down into his soul it went worming, no wake behind it, no dragging lines, no loose wheel at the helm, but straight into his soul. Two days later, when she picked up the chair and put it back in the same exact position, as she had done on every occasion, Badger Martineau knew something occult, strange, perhaps forbidden, was working on him through the innocence of his grandchild. The sense of displeasure grew.

"Alexa, why do you put that little rocker back in the same place all the time?" The old Morris chair creaked and groaned beneath his shifting body as he looked at her kneeling at the dollhouse. For a moment her joy seemed part of the structure.

Like cookies from the jar her eyes looked, wide and spontaneous and yet something else in them, alerting him. To what? Was it her absolute charm? Her sudsy clean innocence and naïveté? Above all, the woman. "Doesn't it belong there, Grampa? I'm the housekeeper. Dime a day, remember?" Her way was inscrutably honest, direct, and innocent. The blonde tresses were neatly tied into a small bun on top of her head and her cheekbones leaped out under those fair eyes. "All the other things, the beds, the bureaus, the rugs, the other chairs, can be any place. They

149

belong any place. I think this chair belongs here." It was the housekeeper's decision, the housekeeper's_move, and a bit of sass in the words. With an outstretched hand, her head twisting back to look at him, words in her eyes, her index finger with the touch of the house mistress, put the old rocking chair in its place at the bedroom window, the river and the sea beyond it for sure. A relationship was being cemented, and Badger was thinking that she could do it with her eyes closed, when a long forgotten scene came back on him, clear as Irish crystal in Mother's cabinet.

In one startling moment the old sea captain Badger Martineau saw his own grandfather, the great elder Tilmon Martineau, seaman too, bearded, calling from the chair at the window. "Look, sonny boy, there comes The Lady Esmerelda off her cruise. Six, maybe seven months now. There'll be jawing and pouring and empty cups this night for Smithson and his crew. I hope the old boy comes by to pay his respects. I took him on his first cruise. Damn well better!" He had leaned forward in his chair, the cane under his chin, one leg under that chin, the other leg off yet in the depths of the China Sea.

It was so clearly enacted it shook him down to his heel. And he also saw, in the middle of it, like a black space, a void, there was something missing or hidden that continually gnawed its way at him. Alexa had no part in this, he was positive, but the void, the blackness, was there.

Three days on top of that revelation, Alexa at disruption and reassembling the house, the void was still a spot of anonymity in his mind. She picked up the little rocker, the last piece of furniture on the floor and gently placed it back under the bedroom window, the sea and the river surely beyond that view. Looking back at her grandfather the smile was broad and genuine and full of happiness as if she had accomplished one more gallant or thoughtful deed.

"Does something tell you where to put that chair, Alexa?" His cane was leveled in the air at the room on the second floor, at the rocking chair, and his hand shook but a little as he held the cane as an arrow. The old sailor was aware of other trends and twisting going on about him. For the first time in many years the phantom pain came back from the missing foot, the phantom pain

150

from the phantom foot he had lived with for a monstrous stretch of years. That responsible, deadly storm he could feel again and the wind driving its own fury all across the China Sea and the terror and pain of the spar coming down on his leg. *Oh, Lord, was this sweet child his messenger of death?...* as he thought that spar once was.

"Oh, Grampa, don't be silly. Chairs can't talk. Even if they did, would it be chair talk? Or wood talk? Or furniture talk? Would a little kid like me know it?" That ever-delightful light was in her eyes, in the curve of her lips, as she slowly gave a look to her grandmother looking from another room. Her hip swung out in a sudden stance, the woman in the child. Oh, he had seen such things in his long life. He remembered her mother in a moment of silver flashes at the back of his head; whole scenes of her wrapped in the magic and joy of her own young days...and his. *No, not this child!* Yet he could see his own daughter with a face so dirty and black he could see but her eyes and her teeth, and the widest grin of all across her face. Caught he was in sense and apparition, time swelling and contracting, strange winds indeed. Back into the contour of the Morris chair he went, nestling, waiting for...*for whatever*.

What was it she had said; *A dime a day, just for pennies.*

There it came, in another flash of coin, that other coin from so long ago, his hand reaching into his grandfather's open purse on that very windowsill, taking the gold piece, slipping it into his pocket. He had told his pal Knack Courtis about the clutch of coins and Knack had told him he'd give him tons of pennies for one of the gold ones. Knack had a way of promising the moon, had magic on his tongue, bore deception in his heart. It was easy sliding it into his pocket and slipping out of the house with it. All hell had broken loose at home when the coin was discovered missing. Not a soul offered up Badger's name. It was unthinkable that the godly child would steal from his beloved grandfather.

And the weight of the coin hung on him for years, until his grandfather was gone. Somewhere at sea, under Trade Winds, in the terror of The Horn, that weight was dispatched, it seemed, forever. Now another child had found it and brought it back. God, how foolish had he been. Knack was, at length, nothing but a

151

conniver, a thief. Badger wondered what had happened to the coin. Knack, it was said, was known to have amassed many coins in his day.

So it was, after added weeks of recall, the displeasure coming alive when only Alexa was in the room, at the dollhouse, at that chair, that Badger Martineau began seeking information about Knack Courtis. Knack, he found out from the milkman, had died in a train crash in Idaho a good dozen years earlier. But there was a daughter living in the next town.

Perhaps there could be some atonement, even at this stage of the game.

"I'm sorry to disturb you, Ma'am, my name is Badger Martineau. I knew your father a long time ago. I know that he collected coins and wonder if that collection is still extant. One of my favorite coins might well have been in that collection."

"I know of you, sir. I know of your daughter and some of your sons. My father left few things. Property, mostly. He had come into possession of a large parcel of land out west when the train accident happened. The train went right off the bridge. I think just about everybody on board was killed."

Badger relented and told her the truth about her father's promise, about the gold coin, about the disappointment. "I think it was a 1905 gold ten-dollar piece. That small theft haunted me for years. I think it has come back again." He told Knack's daughter about Alexa's place in all of it, about the chair, about dimes and pennies, about some kind of relentless pursuit now coming on him. About his doubts and his true considerations.

"I have some few things of father's, in boxes mostly, one old trunk I haven't looked into for years, Mr. Martineau. I promise I will look. 1905, you say?"

"Aye, 1905, a shine you wouldn't believe."

A week later, a knock at the door, and Knack Courtis' daughter Pamela came to his chair. A huge smile was on her face. In her hand she held a shining ten-dollar gold piece. It sat in the palm of her hand like a token straight from Fort Knox. It caught the slanting sunlight as though its surface had been a mirror, the way a wayward coin in the gutter might catch the early sunlight, at a slant, as an eye catcher for an early walker.

152

Pamela took everything in. She saw a sudden change in the one-legged old man locked into an old Morris chair, his beard egret-white, a gnarled cane hanging on the back of the chair. She caught her breath when she saw the dollhouse in the front room, the beautiful child kneeling at it, the furniture strewn about but being re-assembled one room at a time. The little girl turned and smiled at her. Pamela swore that they were exchanging a secret, that knowledge of everything possible and true was crossing between their eyes.

Knack's daughter was a happy woman when she left Badger Martineau's house. The old man had fallen asleep in his chair. The child Alexa had charmed her until her mother had come to take her home. Pamela had some new friends.

And she had one old friend that she called on the telephone when she got home. He was an old classmate. He owned a coin shop a few miles away.

"It was perfect, Sebastian, just like it was the very same coin from out of the past. I thank you, for an old man and for a lovely little girl who plays with the dollhouse her grandfather made many years ago. They are a most happy pair."

The Man with a Broken Crutch

It was where the Dark Forest runs out of breath and the river, pretending to be a thief, steals much of daylight's silver. Here one morning, a man with a broken crutch came out of the forest and went along the river gathering its coin. He wore a cap for the weather and a jacket Time had touched roughly. And he limped.

The limp was a serious limp, almost twisting the man's frame. His left foot had a dragging stutter to it and the boot was greatly worn. The man looked as if he would topple easily. And need or want moved in the air about him.

The single crutch at his left side was crude and bound in places, where it had been broken, with tightly coiled wire. Avershaw the blacksmith, from his porch, saw him first, noticed how he leaned to one side. "Melba," he called, and his wife came onto the porch. "We will have another for breakfast," he said. Her apron was gathered in her hands and she looked at the stranger and said, "I am sure we will."

Avershaw, a big man with red suspenders and heavy corduroy pants, stood and hailed the other man. "Could you stand for coffee and a biscuit, sir? We do not have much but we can ease some of your hunger. Eggs would be another matter." Again Avershaw noted how the man leaned almost to the point of falling. Then he saw the man's kindly face, the clear blue eyes, and the way he held his chin. And his hands! His hands were delicate and smooth and did not look as if they belonged with the crutch or had used the crutch for a long time.

"You are too kind, sir," the man with the crutch said. A slight smile wore on his face. "We are in luck, for I have two eggs here I found last evening in the forest, and no place to cook them." From a pocket of the worn jacket he brought out two brown eggs that could be yet idling in a nest. "If the lady of the house would oblige, she may do as she wishes with them." He held out the two brown eggs and Avershaw called his wife. "Melba, we'll have biscuits dipped in eggs today, just the way you like them."

Then Avershaw pointed to a chair and said, "Rest easy while the biscuits get dipped and fried. We'll have our coffee here

154

where the sun comes first. If I were a carpenter I would fix that crutch for you, but my iron would be too heavy for you." Then Avershaw said, "By what name are you called, sir?"

"They call me Stick. They have called me Stick for a long time, for so long I know no other name. So Stick I will be. It is not uncomfortable for me."

They ate their biscuits with a small mound of butter and sweet syrup. And a second cup of coffee.

"Do you have far to go?" Avershaw said, as he finished his coffee. "We could put some lunch in a bag for you."

"Not far," Stick said, "not far at all."

When the coffee was gone Stick said thank you and went on his way.

Just before noon, still where the forest runs out of breath and the river steals daylight, Stick was hailed by another man in his front yard. The man had seen the man's serious limp in the heat of the sun. "Stranger, would a bit of shade and a small bite of food aid you on your journey? We do not have much, but we will share. I am here with my two daughters. Today is a day without meat for us. We have a few pennies left from bread we bought."

"Such a lucky day it is," Stick said. "Last night in the forest I came upon a deer who had recently impaled himself. I came away with some venison." From deep in his jacket pocket he drew out a small parcel wrapped in dark paper. "However your daughters choose to cook it, let it be done." The daughters danced away with the venison. Soon the aroma climbed on the air in the middle of the day. And there was a sauce to go with the bread and the four of them dipped their bread and ate the venison.

"My name is Rastoff and I am a music teacher," Rastoff said, his big teeth showing as he talked. "If I could work with wood, I would make you a new crutch to assist you in your journey. But I have no knowledge of wood. Nor what its grain is or where its strength lies, except here." And with that he drew a violin up from below the table and played songs for Stick and his daughters. After a while, Stick said, "I must be going. But I do not have far to travel." He left with his *thank you* as soft as music on the air.

Stick was not far away by the close of evening. A young

boy came up to him and said, "My mother saw you coming for a long time from her window. We do not have much, but you are welcome to eat at our table. We have soup. It is thin soup, but it will be warm."

"Young man," Stick said, "tell your mother we are in luck. Just last evening, in the middle of the Dark Forest, where there was a small patch of late sunlight, I found two potatoes, two beets and two carrots." He dug deep into his jacket pocket and brought out the vegetables. "Tell your good mother to thicken the soup with these."

The boy nodded with delight and ran off to give the vegetables to his mother. He soon came back and said, "She thanks you a great deal. If my father were here he could fix your crutch for you, but he is away in the Great War that moves around the world. We hope he comes back soon. He is a carpenter and could fix your crutch easily."

At dusk they ate the newly thickened soup with the potatoes and the beets and the carrots cut up in it. The soup was delicious and the boy soon fell asleep on the porch of his house while the mother cleaned the dishes. Stick said goodbye. "I have to keep moving. You have a fine boy. I hope your husband gets back soon. War is a great separator, but often not the final one."

His way took him along a stone wall for a few miles, the sun sinking all the while.

The river had nearly given up all of its daylight when Stick was walking past an old farmhouse sitting back from the road like a deep shadow. Not one window had a light in it, nor was there any smoke coming from the chimney. A voice hailed him from the darkness in front of the house. "If you have no place to sleep, sir, we could put you up, but you must be able to do with the darkness and the cold. We do not have any light or any kindling to start a fire or any matches for that matter. I am afraid that my children will not be able to do their reading this night and they might also catch cold. The edge of the moon says it is going to be cold."

"You are most kind, sir," Stick said, "but fear not. Last evening in the forest I found some flint and stone in an old pouch on a tree stump. We can start a fire with them."

"All well and good," the man in the darkness said, "but we

still have no kindling to get the big logs burning."

"Ah, but we do, "Stick said, as he slammed his broken crutch over a large stone in the wall and splintered it for kindling. The sound crackled so harshly in the night it frightened the man.

"But how will you walk on the morrow?" the man said.

Stick had no hesitation. "You will make me a crutch tonight," he replied.

"I have been unable to work for a long time," the man said. But all night he worked hard on several pieces of wood he found behind his house, knowing that before this stranger came he would not have even looked for such wood. Light came from a good fire and warmth filled the house and the children were asleep after reading their lessons. In the morning the man handed Stick a shiny new crutch that caught the early morning sun all along its shaft. The crutch was smooth with a lacquer finish on it and a pad on the top where it fit under Stick's arm.

That sun was barely up over the horizon when Stick walked away in the early rays of sunlight. Down past the fields he went, past the stone walls, to where the river again was catching up all the daylight it could grasp. Once, with his new crutch, he waved back at the man.

Later that evening all the people gathered in town and were talking about the man with the broken crutch.

"I am glad that we were able to feed him," Avershaw said, his thumbs hooked on his red suspenders. "We gave him breakfast, a royal breakfast, a meal to begin the day with." He paused, hooking his suspenders a little higher. "As my mother used to say, 'A meal to touch the backbone.'"

"And we gave the poor man his lunch," Rastoff said, "with venison and thick gravy. A meal also fit for a king." He smiled proudly, his large teeth showing. "We even played music for him to soothe his vagrant soul. If there were a place for that poor man to live, this would be it. We all did so much for him. All taking our turn with a stranger." Those around him nodded in agreement.

The boy's mother, not to be outdone, not wanting to be left out of a share of goodness, took her turn. "A most splendid and thick soup we gave the man. Thick as any soup can be, with potatoes and beets and new carrots to give solid offerings. A treat

157

for any beggar on his rounds. The kind that sticks to one's ribs." It was a kind of punctuation when she added, "And he ate a goodly share of it."

The others nodded in agreement again, seemingly all of one mind.

They were very satisfied with themselves, puffed and self-indulgent, but a voice from the edge of light, the man from the darkness, said, "Do any of you know what he gave to us? Why do we continually wrap ourselves up in our own gifts? Why do we tie up our own ribbons in such a manner?"

"Well," the boy's mother said, "what did you do for him? It was near dark when he left my house."

"What fools we are, "the man answered. "It's not what we did for him. It's what he did for us. He took care of us. Me, a useless man for years, I made a crutch for him. I haven't worked like that in a long time and I guess we all know that." For a moment he hung his head. "That's one of the reasons he came here. The man needed a crutch to get on with. And he saw to it that I made it for him. We did not really do for him. He did for us, but we are afraid to say it."

The next morning, on the other side of the river, where the mountain suddenly stands tall and the field stops its long run, the man with a broken crutch came limping out of the forest ready to lean on some more people.

An elderly man, enjoying early sunlight, hailed him from his porch.

Two Characters Caught Up
in Chapel Town

*Judd Helme, as a youngster, was held by his naked heels
out over the edge of this very same bridge by his drug-addicted
father, and in front of his mother, now long deceased. The act was
done in view of a small group of onlookers, one of whom related
to me the events of that situation. Nobody knows why Judd was not
dropped. It was only after a considerable amount of time, and
rehabilitation, that the witness was able to tell me the
circumstances, he too being hit by the slam-bang of it all, he too
taking a look down into that awful reflection... thinking, as he
often said, that memory comes in most horrid shapes, and most
horrid visages.*

No one can tell this story about Judd Helme but me. I am
the cartographer, the journalist, the diarist in all these movements,
scenes and words, these tokens of time. You'll have to trust me
and my place in all of it. So I tell it now, watching from where I
have always watched, eagle-eyed yet custodial, making it fit the
present. I do not have a telephone or a television, but my view is
peerless; I live on the other hill above the Coolichee River and the
bridge that spans it.

I see everything the river knows.

The river tells me everything it knows.

It happens again today, the memory leap. I can see
everything converging.

Another street person, from up on the hill, from up at
Chapel Town, old Pere Gargan, pushes along the bridge his
shopping carriage loaded with who-knows what, tatters and
ribbons and rags blowing in the wind, perhaps junk *per se*.
Discredited he looks, to say the least, and dirty, one glance saying
he is soiled in raiment and person and has been that way for a long
spell. But he is not yet ill at ease in any truly social manner. Now
and then he puffs and blows on gloveless hands. Irreverent and
irresponsive, it seems, he comes up behind old acquaintance and
fellow streeter Judd Helme dangling in a threatening lean over the
rail of the bridge over the Coolichee River, not far inland from the
old Atlantic itself.

159

He's as cool as the day is, old Gargan, almost soft-shoeing along the paved surface of the bridge. No hurry to his pace, ambivalent in his approach, always ambivalent, how he manages.

Judd Helme's leaning over the rail is treacherous, *I know. I see it.* He is leaning again into dare and history, into doubt and the future. You'd figure he's obviously in somber contemplation, it appears, but has been seen by the old French relic in the same posture on several other occasions. Pere Gargan has read Judd's mind in those instances for sure. It is not unlike his own mind in part, or like his used to be. Judd, he knows, hears the click of infinity as well as he hears the clack of the carriage's damn-near-square wheel. Both must sound like old single shot rifle bolts slamming home, attention coming in the ranks. Pere knows it, the before and the after.

I can say this: it's as if I hear the same echoes each of them hears in their contemplation. It's pealing and illustrious. It's musical. And I steal it. Like a sound painting. One of the Masters. I'm a thief of thoughts, you see. My argument is credulous; if I hear the river, and what it knows, I hear everything. And I hear the river.

I know: mild November comes atop them in grayness and the square wheel announcing the carriage also carries the *tink-tink* of returnable cans and click of glass bottles, the cluttering rattle of them bound with meager promise. These are Pere Gargan's mild economics in slow motion... tinkle and crawl of them, penny push of them, pocket stash. High and low he's been in search, behind brush and billboard, barrel and cache; now, at a nickel a piece, it is worthy effort. As a child he was grounded in this work, at two cents a piece in youthful days; all glass bottles of pop, tonic, soda, name it what you will at synonymy. Yet it was the feel of the bottle, long before cans came along; the touch he remembers, the cylindrical till at hand, now and then a weapon of one sort or another, Time deciding which, darkness or an alley often a decider too.

I know: Gargan himself, like Helme, is also more than nondescript. He is more than looking older than he is, more than usually destitute. But he breathes in a normal manner, and betrays no surprise in the words he tosses out, as if he were solely the

160

dealer of cards. His walk is not impeded by thought or utterance, that musical soft-shoe some people go through life with. He struts on his way, the tongue loose with its barbs, loaded with irony's juices, coated with the phlegm of acidity. "Wait until tomorrow, Judd," Gargan yells out in mock terror as he moves across the bridge, his palms up suddenly in plenitude, past the out-leaning Helme. He could have said, *You had one chance before*, but offered, "No turkey down there, Judd. No stuffing and gravy and mashed potatoes down there today, Judd. No asparagus spears or cranberry red for you, Judd." One hand, turned from offertory, rolls across his sparse midsection in mild mockery, one hand in half salute. Does he pretend he doesn't remember all of this?

I hear: his voice sail out over the river. The carriage wheel clacks out the caesura, a breath caught in place. "Oh, my boy," Gargan adds at stressful punctuation, "wait until tomorrow." Too, there is an air of rampant but coached disdain in his tone. He could be kidding; he could be not. "Today is Thanksgiving and they'll give us a meal fit for kings. Believe me on that. That's a little later today, with a little head bowing, of course, and a little begging, the kind they always expect from us. Behaving like what they are. Believing like what we do. Take it from me, I say; believe it. If they do nothing else, they'll put out a meal fit for kings, the prayers and *thank yous* included as part of the humanitarian way, of course." Then, clucking, ducking his head as if avoiding a tossed rotten egg, he adds, "Or should I say in a *humilitarian* way?" He titters, walks off as if he were a ticket collector at a theater line, once again knowing how the scene behind him unfolds itself, the unsaid gesture, the stationary word.

I hear: the wheel clacking again as Pere heads uphill, his simple task and directive just about concluded. He yells again in his retreat, the small breeze playing the beard on his face, "Get wet tomorrow, Judd. Tomorrow's soon enough." Tittering, self-pleased, pleasant, immune to response of any order, he waves backwards over his head, which lolls in self-admiration, acceptance, a point made. He could have brushed his hands off at a job well done. The limp knocking at his right leg is in concert with the square wheel. Life has its edges, it says, even for the halt and the lame.

I know: in his turn, Judd eyes the cool water once more, alert to the magnetic pull. He is suddenly aware, by warmth of his fingers, that the lint in his pocket bottoms is grainy and not wooly, like course sand, or some ferric remnants, perhaps a cache of sorts rusting away so near his body, catching at sweat, coming up off-orange in color. He digs in a corner, feels the thread line, thumb-rolls a small piece back into soft but measurable reality as dry as a rolled snot. *Dust unto dust,* an old voice says to him. It is not the philosopher-with-old-carriage's punctuation. It is another voice, from another realm.

I see: Judd watches the man and the carriage as it heads uphill.

I knew: earlier, again, for one bare moment out on the bridge over the Coolichee River, the skies filled with snow's threat, endless gray in every direction, Judd Helme smelled himself, at first in mild disdain. Then it became a loud wake-up call. Christ, Judd thinks, he could have made himself sick. He didn't like his own smell, almost vile. The odors, ranks and ranks of them, assailed him, rising certain as steam or vapor, his nose separating, cataloguing. He couldn't remember how many times he'd thought of making the jump from the bridge over the river when all existence came at him in irreparable bounds. Dumpster smells stabbed him, damp alleys, how many old loading docks he had slept under in the company of rats, now and then a slob of a woman pushing herself at him, her dress linens like stained grain bags, eyes at memory, a leg hooking his leg and a hand groping, Mother Earth at her poorest. Time with its worst odor, and spent, spent, spent. He looks again at the provided mirror of the river. He has a sudden aversion to that singular reflection from the river face. It's been there forever. It calls his name as well as his face.

I know: all of that, from my position on the hill, through reconstruction of facts; but the mirror leaps up at him from the still waters of the Coolichee now that the wind is low, the current slow and slack, his mind moving at the edge of trance often self-induced, or having significant other cause.

I would assume: it is an unexciting existence Judd benignly sees in the portrait, the image; there is little else on either surface to come at him, the river's or his mind's. His life has been so: in

162

school he was average, mediocre in all efforts, cheating now and then, failing at any and all athletics; in the army also, where he served without distinction, never volunteering, never stepping forward, content to follow the man ahead of him. Now and then, drawn by a faint impression of thoughts long gone, he remembers the hollow sound of a bugle call might well have come across the desert sand to him, but it never really beckons him, though the music of a few notes still hangs in the back of his head, which he dubs lazy nostalgia. The one stripe he earned in the army was only decided by time spent in one grade and kicked onto another. Only poor, lonely Fred Glibbers' face comes to him from any assembly of comrades, he too a lost soul, the two of them as if marooned on a small island of selves by the vast organization of the army loosed at Desert Storm. Judd wonders why he remembers a bit of Fred Glibbers' face, nothing else being left of the man; he sees the face in the reflection of the Coolichee River all the time, or every time he has hung over the edge of the bridge. He thinks, *It is a rare thing when a lost image tries to resurrect itself.*

Judd knows Pere Gargan's passing voice is the age of experience talking to him, most directly, most truly. The clack of the wheel passes on, fades away. Pere Gargan, for all his intent and purpose, is once again ghostly. The deliverance fits him.

In Chapel Town, Judd Helme has discovered a place where he can sleep each night without being rousted during the night or too early in the morning and forced to move on. He has found a place where he fits. But the days of Chapel Town seem numbered. Officials, never enamored by the cluster of blue and gray tents on city confines (the unpaved inner-city parking lot on the upper hill), are pushing to close the camp as soon as they can.

As long as his abode is standing, Helme believes he will not leave. At those moments he affirms he will not jump from the bridge, the magnet forever.

"I will stay here until I am shoved out," Helme once vowed. He is aged, forty-years old but looking sixty, folded, bent, pruned-up, arthritic in minor joints. He is a former laborer at bricks, stones, gravel of Mother Earth. He is one of those 100 or so people hanging on to their last foothold at Chapel Town. "Perhaps we'll be driven out at the point of a bayonet. But we are

163

not homeless. We have these homes. We have a place with a name." There were times he could feel the force of the argument, but not always.

Each time Judd walks away from the waters of the Coolichee, he goes directly to the collection of shacks, tents, and quick-saved blow-downs of Chapel Town, filled with the only people he knows. Those who live there have given the place its name. Chapel Town is more than a collection of lost souls in quick cover: it is communal living at imagination's widest extension. It is a place where prayers are tenants at all hours, as well as bitching, a hum that one can hear in the near-silent darkness or at high noon, that predicts a word like *susurrus* with the same hum. People do not need to pack up and leave every day, lugging their belongings through the streets on stolen grocery carts, as they did when they lived down in lower city shelters.

Everything in life, to Helme's view, is rag tag, nondescript, and yet ageless. He thinks of Gargan's shopping carriage, the image of it, how it moves almost a load of nothing to almost a place that is nowhere. None of the people of the cluttered commune have anywhere to go. Yet he dreams of a goodness he cannot create in his waking hours, a hope shorn of its roots yet waiting to be caught.

Of the lot of them in Chapel Town, Judd Helme believes himself the most homeless and the most broken. Staring down at the water of the Coolichee River has always made him feel that way, and almost always exposes the hidden thoughts of his mind. The water bounces visions back to him in traces of oil, slicks full of color, separations of some order too distant to be known. Those sensations come along with him like fabled scars or the most personal baggage, clutching, or having handles for constant grasping, toting a lifetime. There are moments where such weights might crush him. That ominous pressure he feels, oversize rocks in place. Pain, anger, frustration itself, are made of iron the bearer cannot release. Water below has no temperature, no touch of freeze, no choke hold on air's passage. It is just another dimension, another level looking for a new name. It may say elsewhere or newness or escape. It might never say hello because it would be the grand goodbye.

Old Gargan knows what he's talking about; that's experience for you, dragged as baggage out of Korea, the Philippines, a dozen old camps and stations of his life. Occasionally, in the soft halt of a day, past a quick drink or a mouthful of tuna on a roll, his memory scratches at bits and pieces left over from the last bout with nostalgia. *I've been everywhere,* he says; *I've been everywhere.* He can see the face of the singer but long ago lost the name. He sees a train speeding at him down the miles of Kansas fields or Missouri plains. A small, quiet, old town lunges at him; a face flies up from beside the tracks. Eyes are caught pretty blue, the mouth is rose red and wet, and the night folds again around them. Her name is, perhaps, Mary or Madeleine. She wants what is not hers, too young to own it for good. Ownership and promise came for one night, a lifetime of promise. Then, shantied for sleep, desperate at new dreams, a shotgun pries at his ribs, steers him down the tracks to jump another freighter heading out of life. He'd been posted close to death innumerable times, yet here he is pushing a shopping carriage with one square wheel, that quiet old town too far down the tracks to come back; *I am noisy, here I come. Listen to what I say. I am death's slave, shackled forever to meagerness. Here I go.*

If you jump now, someone eats your meal. It's that simple; someone else eats your meal; someone won't go hungry.

He says to an acquaintance at the edge of camp, "Don't worry, Judd won't jump or fall. Not today, anyway. I know that boy, right from the very beginning, through all the travails become and begot. A whole lifetime gets squeezed in on a person and if you don't grab at it and hold on at the beginning, it will haunt you forever. That's the good Lord's truth. Rivers never lie. Never lie. They move the silence around you. They tote your barge and lift your bail, but you're never free of your first river. I know that and Judd knows that. How many times you figure he's looked at that damn water looking back at him, the Coolichee taking a stab at him, leaving this long impression? How many times since it first looked up at him? The eyes becoming the eyes, the nose becoming the nose, all that identity clearer to the river than to that young kid dangling forever. We don't know and he won't know. It won't be

165

any closer than that first time the river looked back at him, looked him right in the eye, saying his name over and over again. His hunger must be stronger than his fear of death. And we'll have cranberry sauce to boot."

I see: after the Thanksgiving meal, the cranberry gone, the thank yous and amens made slightly tolerable, Pere Gargan takes Judd Helme's place at the rail, assumes his son, jumps.

About the Author

Tom Sheehan is the author of twelve books. *Brief Cases, Short Spans* was published in November 2008 by Press 53. *Epic Cures*, won a 2006 IPPY Award. *A Collection of Friends* was nominated for the Albrend Memoir Award. Sheehan has also been nominated for nine Pushcart Prizes, three Million Writers, a Noted Story of 2007, and received the Georges Simenon Award for Fiction. He served in Korea in 1951-52.